LOVE with ANYONE but YOU

Love With Anyone But You

Linda Becker

Seeker Publishing

Seeker Publishing 2018

First Printing: 2018

ISBN: 978-0-578-20189-4

Seeker Publishing

O'Fallon, MO

Chapter 1

It was a bright, clear September day—unusual for Atlanta—but she didn't notice. As she walked down the sidewalk, returning from her doctor's appointment, all Kate could think about was what he had told her. "I'm truly surprised," the doctor said. "I really thought the treatment would work, but it hasn't." *You're surprised?* Kate thought to herself. *I'm thirty-nine years old, unmarried, no kids, and the Grim Reaper just popped his head in to tell me it's time to go already! Surprised doesn't even begin to cover this!*

Kate had done her best to act bravely while she sat in his office, and he told her to prepare for her life to end. Only six months ago she'd gone in for some extensive tests after experiencing unusual pains that she could no longer explain away. Earlier in the year she thought it was gas—at the worst maybe an ulcer. But as the pains grew worse, she decided she needed a good checkup. Little did she realize that it would reveal advanced liver cancer that was showing signs of spreading to other parts of her body, and nothing seemed to be able to stop it. She had tried some experimental drugs in the last seven weeks, but she had displayed no improvement. Her options diminished before her eyes, with every word from her doctor's mouth. She had weeks—weeks to enjoy the fortieth year of her life. She would never live to celebrate its completion. What was she supposed to do with that?

"Kate, I'm sorry. There's nothing we can do." The doctor's words kept playing over and over on a loop in her mind. Dr. Kent had been terrific all the way through this voyage of discovery. He was a rock of strength and a bank full of knowledge on her disease. Oh! There it was again, "There's nothing we can do." The phrase slapped her in the face once again. *Was it real? Did it really happen? Could I please wake up and find out I don't have to go through this? I don't want to die! I don't want to let go! I'm just not ready!*

It was baffling to her that she could become this ill at such a young age. Kate had always been extremely careful about what she ate. She exercised every day. She had given up fast food years ago. To say she was a health food fanatic would hardly begin to describe her. She carefully scrutinized everything she ate for fat content, calories, additives, and—most importantly—cleanliness. Germs, bacteria, illness, infection—these were all opportunities available to the one who ingested the wrong morsel. It was a constant battle, but one she waged constantly and consistently to protect herself from becoming the victim of these merciless, invisible, and silent killers. But it was not only her diet that Kate expected to be pristine. There was a certain order, consistency, and sanitization that encompassed her entire life. She expected everything to be the way she wanted it and when she wanted it. Being diagnosed with terminal cancer had not only declared her defeat, but it had really thrown a wrench into her extremely organized plan.

She thought back to Dr. Kent again. He had really been kind to her. Of course he had! He wasn't the one dying! She pictured him asking her, "Kate, now is the time to think about what you want to do most with your life. What's on your bucket list? You need to think about your loved ones and making peace." He had become more than just a doctor. He was her friend—her confidant and counselor.

As a result of holding a strict criterion for everything and everyone in which she came into contact, Kate had very few friends. People were afraid to get too close to her for fear of feeling like a disappointment. Kate really didn't mind though. She was perfectly content without casual friendships. She didn't see much use in them. Her life flowed with the consistency of perfectly strained broth and delivered just as much excitement. Excitement wasn't for Kate. She didn't like surprises, drama, or emotional rollercoasters. She was happy with a modest, programmed, and hygienic life. And she shared this life with a steady boyfriend who was—in her eyes—more seamless than she was—Tom.

Tom was tall, dark, and devastatingly handsome. He wasn't the body-builder type, but he was in great physical shape. He had thick, dark hair and icy blue eyes that made her tremble the first time she saw him. In fact, she was quite amazed when she found out that he was attracted to her. While Kate was not ugly, she was very plain. She rarely wore any makeup and she kept her hair in an easily maintained pageboy style for convenience. She couldn't imagine why Tom would want to date her, when he could surely have his pick of any woman in Atlanta—probably the whole state of Georgia. Nevertheless, they had stayed together for seven years in an uncomplicated, uncommitted, homogenous relationship without a single argument or breakup.

Kate felt little beads of sweat break out along her forehead as the words "bucket list" and "make peace" passed through her brain. She looked up at the sun streaming down through the tree branches above. Fortunately there were so many trees downtown to give some respite from the intense heat. As usual, she was wearing black, which only made it worse. She hoped she could make it back to the air conditioning before she had become sweaty.

She crossed the street and walked into the building where she worked. Her fellow employees were just coming back after their lunch breaks. She looked around at them engaging in chit-chat and joking about needing a nap. She listened to them with resentment in her thoughts. She'd never cared about any of them as long as she had worked there, but today she wished she could be any one of them instead of herself. She wanted to be laughing and giggling and have nothing more on her mind than going home tonight to her boyfriend.

Tom! What was she going to tell Tom? The thought hit her like a downtown bus. She didn't want him to worry about her. She could do enough worrying for both of them. She'd kept her doctor visits a secret until she was sure it was nothing. Now, it was something. The time for shielding him had come to an end. She had to find a way to tell him.

She would go home tonight and probably find Tom cooking some dinner for them both. He loved to cook, so he would let himself into her house after work and whip up some incredible dish that put restaurants to shame. She hated to cook and was happy to have him do it. Understanding how flavors went together to make a meal was not one of her skills, and she despised handling raw meat. The thought of all that bacteria in her kitchen and on her hands was too much to bear. It was much easier to let Tom handle it and not think about it. Besides she was always there with the cleanup, sanitizing the countertops and appliances with her antibacterial cleaners in tow. Together, they made a great team. Yes, she and Tom fit together like cleansers and rubber gloves.

In all this time Tom had never once suggested that they move in together, but he was at her house most of the time. He maintained a very nice apartment downtown, which gave him a chance to give them both some space when necessary. Not that they had ever required any space from each other. They were very much in sync when it came to their likes and dislikes. First of all Tom was very neat and understood Kate's need for cleanliness. They also both adored alternative jazz but despised any kind of sports. The main reason Tom kept the separate quarters was his job. He worked in real estate, and sometimes that meant crazy hours. Tom was much more social than Kate was. There were a lot of networking gatherings he attended without her—thankfully. Having the apartment allowed him to come and go without disturbing her sleep routine. Kate appreciated his thoughtfulness and the respect he held for her needs.

She pictured Tom standing at the stove when she came through the door that night, and she wondered how she was going to find the words necessary to tell him her news. She walked into her office and fell into her chair. She leaned back and closed her eyes imagining him standing in front of her. She saw herself saying it in different ways, but none of them seemed like the right way to tell someone she was dying. She was contemplating how to use Google for ideas on how to have such a conversation, when she was startled by her office phone buzzing.

She pressed the button and said hello. Her boss was on the line. "Kate, got a second?"

"Sure," she answered. "I'm on my way." She picked up her appointment book and headed to her boss's office. Kate was a sales rep for a fragrance manufacturer. She'd been with the company for eight years and really enjoyed what she did. It was a small company—only twenty-three people. She liked it that way. Not because it gave her a warm, fuzzy, family feeling. She really didn't care anything about her fellow coworkers, but she liked the fact that there were very few people for her to deal with on a daily basis. It meant that the restrooms were cleaner, because they had little traffic. It meant fewer names that she needed to remember. It was just another phase of her life that fit into her need for complete control of her environment.

Kate was not friendless or completely cut off from her fellow employees. For the most part, she coexisted quite nicely with everyone in her office, which made operations run smoothly. There was only one person on staff whom she could not stand, and oddly enough, he was Tom's best friend. In fact, he had been the one who actually introduced her to Tom seven years ago. For the life of her, though, she could never understand how the two of them would be friends. Ben was crude, obnoxious, overweight, immature, and basically a repulsive human being in the eyes of Kate. But she would forever be grateful that Ben had brought Tom into their offices all those years ago, or they might never have met. Consequently, she endured Ben's childish, comedic stunts and disgusting behavior out of agonizing obligation.

She stepped into her boss' office. Hank was not the kind of man you would envision running a fragrance company. He was entering his eighties. His short, white hair usually looked as though he'd just dragged his fingers through it while in heavy thought, which was most likely the case. He still wore dark, plastic-framed glasses from the 1960's, which gave him a sort of Spencer Tracy appeal. And although he was a little rough around the edges, he still always wore a shirt and necktie every day to work. He looked more like an editor of a newspaper than a maker of aromatherapy, but she adored him. Kate's parents had been killed in a car wreck when she was in college, so Hank was the closest thing she had to a father. Now she was going to have to find a way to tell him her news, too. It would have to wait though. She still needed time for it to sink into her own mind before she began telling anyone else. She sat down in front of his desk and said, "So what's up, boss?"

Hank sighed heavily. Uh-oh, she thought. He looked up at her with wide eyes and a forced smile, and said, "Good news. I've got a potential client out in Marina Del Rey. He's shopping around for a new supplier and he's very interested in us. I want you to fly out there and talk to him. Sell him on working with us. He'll like you."

"Sure," said Kate. Why did she feel like there was more to this request? Going to see potential new clients was something she did every day. "When do you want me there?" she asked.

"I need you there first thing on the tenth," Hank answered.

"That's Monday," she said.

"That's right. You'll fly out on Sunday afternoon, spend the entire day with him, give him the full treatment, then fly back Tuesday morning," said Hank.

"Okay, boss," she said as she penciled it into her book. Kate started to pull herself up out of her chair, when she heard the other shoe drop.

"Just one more thing…I'm sending Ben with you," Hank said without looking directly at her. He knew she wouldn't take it well.

She sunk back into her chair and observed him. He looked like a dog who knew he'd misbehaved, holding his head low as to avoid a beating. "Ben?" she asked with her face twisted as if she'd just smelled something foul. "Really? Why?" She nervously tucked her hair behind her ears—a habit she'd retained since childhood.

"Yeah, Ben's our best customer service rep. He knows our factory inside out. I'm not saying you don't know what you're doing. You're great. You represent the company very well, but Ben has the facts you need to back up any questions this guy has. Ben knows what this factory is capable of doing and what it can't. I know this guy. He's going to push for everything he can get for his money. Ben will ensure we close the deal."

"Then why not just send Ben?" she asked with a little attitude. Her feelings were just a bit hurt, and she couldn't help but let it show. Besides, the thought of spending travel time with Ben just made her nauseous. Or was it her medication? No, it was Ben.

10

"Because Ben…well…you know. Just look at him. Would you buy anything that guy was selling?" Hank shook his head. "Come on. I really need you and him both for this. You'll make a great team."

Kate quietly nodded her head in the affirmative. She couldn't argue with anything Hank had to say. He was right about all of it. Besides, it was just a couple of days. "Okay, boss. You got it. We'll be on the plane Sunday afternoon." She got up and proceeded to walk out the door.

"Pick up your tickets at the airport. Sally's already ordered them. And for God's sake, get some sun while you're out there," he yelled at her from his chair. "You look white as a ghost and it's the end of summer!"

Kate smiled at his fatherly advice, but tears came to her eyes at the same time. If you only knew, Hank, she thought to herself…if you only knew. She headed back down the hallway to her office.

"Kate!" she heard Ben call from his cubicle. Reluctantly she turned around and popped her head around the corner.

"Yeah?" she said, doing nothing to hide her disappointment.

"So…Marina Del Rey Sunday…that should be cool, huh?" Ben asked smoothly as he rocked back and forth on his heels.

Kate looked at him seriously and said, "Sounds like it could be a very big client. Try not to mess it up." She turned around and headed down the hall.

"I'm looking forward to it, too!" he shouted at her as she walked back to her desk

.

Chapter 2

On Sunday Tom drove both Kate and Ben to the airport. The white, cloudy, overcast sky accurately reflected Kate's demeanor. Kate sat in the front seat, remaining silent, while Tom and Ben conversed for the entire ride. She still could not understand how Tom could endure Ben's immature approach to humor and his obvious disdain for cleanliness. She had drowned out their conversation soon after they had left Ben's apartment. But now she was becoming aware that in place of not listening to them, she had simply wound herself tightly into a wiry ball of anger. She sat there in her seat, twisted and hunched over. The muscles of her face contorted—one eyebrow up slightly higher than the other and the corners of her mouth drawn down so far they almost reached her bony chin. Tom reached his hand over and placed it on hers, which brought her out of her hypnotic state and made her mindful of her clenched jaw. She quickly glanced over at him to see him smiling gently at her, and her scowl evaporated. "Calm down, Kate," she could hear Tom thinking.

At the terminal, Tom kissed her glum face goodbye and said, "Have a good time and try not to look so disappointed. It's just for a couple of days." She could tell that Tom was waiting for her to put a smile on her face. Kate had made it quite clear to him over their years together that she disliked Ben. No, it was more than dislike. She *abhorred* Ben. Abhorred—now there was a word that she could sink her teeth into and chew on for a while! With that happy thought, her mouth pulled out all the stops for a beautiful, toothy grin for Tom. Pleased with her expression, Tom kissed her again and said, "Call me tonight. I'll miss you."

Kate held onto her smile and her hatred. "I'll miss you too," she said. As she looked him directly in the eyes, her hatred melted into sadness. She hadn't the courage to tell Tom anything all weekend, which made this goodbye even harder. With every intention of breaking it to him gently Friday night, she came home to discover he had made reservations at their favorite restaurant. While dining, she became so nervous she could barely eat. Tom kept asking her if something was wrong, but she denied it, and continued to pick at her food. The usual Friday night love-making session make it impossible for her to bring up her cancer after dinner.

Tom worked most of the day on Saturday, and at that point, she knew she wasn't going to tell him. How could she dump that kind of information on her boyfriend and then leave town? No, she had to wait for the right moment and she had to find the right words. *And just what were the right words to tell someone that you're dying?* It was such a depressing conversation to have. *Should she make it humorous?* She pictured herself making up a silly poem, but when she tried to find something that rhymed with *kick the bucket* all she could come up with was…well…something she didn't usually say— although it appropriately expressed her current feelings. It was just such a hard thing for her to wrap her mind around. Saying it out loud made it incredibly real. Secretly she hoped that if she didn't talk about it, then it might just go away. Now she had a few more days to think about it.

She boarded the plane with Ben right alongside her. Kate hated to fly. She wasn't so much afraid of it, as horribly annoyed. Although being suspended in mid-air in a heavy piece of metal didn't meet with her knowledge of science, it was more the concept of public transit that bothered her. Germs thrived in these environments! She didn't like the idea of being locked up with a hundred bacteria-laden humans in a container filled with God-knows-how-many strains of still undiscovered viruses left from the last flight. She tried not to touch any handrails, door handles, or doors as she made her way to her seat. Once seated, she pulled out her anti-bacterial wipes from her purse and wiped down the back of the seat in front of her, the chair arms, and the wall around the window.

Ben watched as she performed her little cleaning ritual. Kate asked as she pulled out a fresh wipe and held it out for him, "Did you want one?"

"No thanks," said Ben. He held out his hands in front of him, palms up. He spit into each palm and then rubbed the saliva into each of his chair arms while he looked straight at her with a smirk on his face. "All done," he said. Then he ran his fingers through the front of his hair and leaned back with a very satisfied, smug look.

Kate watched him in disgust. She pulled out her IPod and stuck the ear buds in her ears all the while not breaking eye contact with him. She leaned back in her seat and closed her eyes. The Xanax she took at home was kicking in. She would do her best to forget that Ben was sitting right next to her.

The flight landed safely in Los Angeles without a hitch. Kate had dozed off listening to her music, but the descent of the plane had brought her back to reality. She glanced over to her left to see Ben looking at her with his usual horrific grin on his face.

"Did you know that you snore?" he asked, still smiling slightly.

Kate wrinkled her brow, moved her seat back to the upright position, and stared straight ahead.

"It's kind of cute, though," he continued. "It's peculiar to hear that kind of noise emanating from your tiny person."

She looked back over at him. "Are you saying I was loud?" she asked quietly, suddenly embarrassed.

"No, not so much loud as…" he struggled for a comparison. "Did you ever see *The Exorcist*?"

Fortunately, the flight attendant made an announcement at that moment for passengers to gather their belongings and make ready to exit the plane. Kate turned her face—which now carried a troubled expression—away from Ben as she scrambled to put her IPod away into her purse. It still baffled her as to why this odd excuse for an adult was traveling with her. She really wondered what her boss was

7

thinking when he sent them on this trip together. Kate breathed a heavy sigh to clear her head, knowing there was no use trying to understand. She would just merely have to accept it and keep going for another twenty-four hours.

On the taxi ride to their hotel, Ben continued to make idle chit-chat, but Kate refused to engage. She just kept thinking about taking a warm bath and falling into a cozy bed. Thoughts like that kept her smiling all the way to their destination.

As they stepped out of the hotel elevator, Ben asked, "Hey, you want to grab a bite to eat? It's still early here, and there's a great view of the…"

"No," said Kate as she unlocked her door. "I'm not hungry." Without looking back she stepped into her room and slammed the door shut.

Once inside her room, she opened up her suitcase and hung her suit in the closet. She took her antibacterial wipes into the bathroom and gave everything a good scouring, including the inside of the tub and shower. She ran a bath and ordered a pot of tea to be sent up. While the bath water was running, she called Tom to let him know that she had arrived safely.

"Hey baby," Tom said as he answered. "Everything go smoothly?"

"Yes, despite the fact that Ben was with me."

Tom laughed. "Oh, come on. Give him a break. He's a good guy."

Kate closed her eyes. The guilty feelings were coming back for not having told him yet about her health. "Tom," she said.

"Yes baby," said Tom.

"I can't wait to see you on Tuesday," she said, frustrated with her lack of intestinal fortitude.

"Me too, baby," replied Tom. "Have a good night. It will be over before you know it."

"Goodnight," she said and hung up the phone.

After her bath, Kate pulled back the sheets on her bed. She reached into her suitcase and pulled out her personal set of sheets she always carried with her on trips. She carefully placed one sheet over the bed and then added the second to use as a barrier between her and the blanket. She threw the hotel pillows on the floor and replaced

8

them with one she had in her suitcase. *You can never be too careful,* she thought to herself as she climbed into bed. She poured herself a cup of tea and switched on the television. Just then a sharp pain ran through her that made her double up. Fortunately she'd been able to fill her prescription for pain meds before she left. She reached over for the bottle on her night table and swallowed it with a gulp of tea. She leaned back on her pillow and closed her eyes. Her mind raced with questions about how she would tell Tom and Hank her news. But all that came to her was a slap of cold hard reality. Like a lightning bolt, the truth flashed before her eyes. She was going to die. *Could this really be happening to me?*

10

Chapter 3

Monday was a success. Ben and Kate met with Jack, the owner of Makes Scents, a popular outlet for personalized fragrances in Marina del Rey. Kate had to admit that Ben was useful on this trip. She was impressed by his knowledge of the fragrance industry and had Jack practically begging to partner with their company by the afternoon. In the taxi on the way back to their hotel Kate thanked Ben for his help making this deal. Ben looked over at Kate. "Thanks for saying that, Kate. I thought we made a really great team today," he said.

Kate thought that could be an overstatement, but she smiled politely and looked out the window of the taxi.

"Hey, let's celebrate tonight!" said Ben. "I know a really nice place to get dinner." Kate looked doubtfully at him. "Come on! Live a little!" said Ben. "I guarantee you'll love it."

Kate wanted badly to just be alone. She'd had so little time to be by herself and digest all that was happening to her. But Ben was right. They were in a beautiful town. They closed the deal. Why not live it up a bit? "Okay. Sounds good," she said. As the words left her mouth, another voice in her head said, "What are you doing?" But it was too late to take it back. She soothed herself with thoughts that she was being a trooper, and Tom would be pleased with her for that.

They stepped out of the cab in front of the hotel and walked together in silence all the way up to their floor. Outside their respective doors, Ben said, "I'll come by your room at six-thirty." Kate nodded back in agreement and shut her door.

As soon as she was in her room, Kate pulled out her trusty anti-bacterial wipes and gave the bathroom another good rub down. She scrubbed with a full smile on her face in the anticipation of a nice, hot soak. With the faucet at full throttle, she sat on the edge of her bed to wait for the tub to fill. She took one of the pain pills from her purse and swallowed it with a glass of water. At this point, the pain was really no more than a nuisance, but according to the doctor, it would continue to increase. Eventually the pills would not be enough. Then she would have no choice but to check into the hospital so they could administer morphine. She closed her eyes and waited for the aching to subside.

After the bath, Kate combed her short dark hair into its familiar page-boy style. She'd always liked her hairstyle and didn't see any reason to change it. It complemented her face shape and it was easy to maintain. Long hair was too much trouble and took up too much time. She felt the same way about makeup. It was too time-consuming. And if there was one thing Kate loved, it was efficiency. She rose every morning at six o'clock to go for a run. Upon returning home, she showered, ate a piece of toast and drank a cup of coffee before scurrying into work at eight. She didn't want anything tying her down or disrupting her schedule.

Ben said it was a nice place so she put on her little black dress and heels. Just as she was putting in her last earring, he knocked on the door. She opened the door to find Ben standing in the hall wearing a short sleeve button down shirt over a pair of gray cargo shorts. Of course, the outfit was not complete without a pair of white socks and Birkenstocks, which he also proudly donned.

His eyes were large as he looked her up and down. "Wow! You look great!" he said. "Ready?"

Kate pulled her chin off the floor from the initial shock of his appearance and replaced it with a sharp scowl.

"What?" he asked. He noticed her eyes inspecting his clothing.

Instead of criticizing him, she said politely, "Maybe I should change," heading back into the room. She wondered what she had to wear that would come close to matching his outfit, other than her pajamas.

"No!" said Ben. "You look great, and I'm starving. Come on!"

Kate breathed a heavy sigh as she followed Ben down the hallway to the elevator. She was tired and hungry and had no energy to fight with him. *It's just a short dinner, and no one knows you in this town,* she placated herself as they descended to the lobby floor. She thought they would hail a cab, but instead Ben insisted that they walk and enjoy the sea air. He convinced her it was only a few blocks. Of course, he wasn't walking in three-inch heels.

As they walked, Ben serenaded her with his review of the day. He complimented her on what a great job she had done with the sale and remarked, once again, just how terrific they were as a team. Kate's feet were throbbing and her ears were thoroughly exhausted from the repetitive sounds coming from her companion. "Are we almost there?" as she interrupted his lengthy monologue. Ben stopped and looked around, "Oh yeah! Here it is! Ha! I was talking so much that I almost walked right past it!"

It wasn't really what you would call a building. It was more like a shack that looked as if it could not survive a stiff wind. Kate halted and looked questioningly at Ben. "This is it!" he said enthusiastically. Kate continued to shift her gaze from him to the shack and back to him. "This is the place? This is the restaurant that you said was such a great place that I had to come here with you?" Kate asked.

"I know. I know," he said. "But it's good. I promise you." He opened the door and gestured for her to enter. The place was crawling with people and Ben pushed her through the crowd. "We've got to make our way to the back. There's usually open tables back there," he shouted over the noise and the music from the jukebox. Kate reluctantly let herself be pushed around the bar, toward the back of the restaurant and silently prayed that he would push her right through the back door.

She saw an empty booth in the corner and she moved toward it. They both slid into the seats. The place was a total dive and Kate made it very evident by the look on her face that she was unimpressed. The waitress came by and Ben ordered two beers for

13

them. "Look," said Ben pointing at the window next to their table. "You can see the water."

"What kind of food do they have here?" Kate shouted across the table.

"This is the best place in California to get authentic Indian food. You're going to love it." Ben said smiling assuredly.

"I don't eat Indian food," she shouted back. "It's too spicy."

Ben rolled his eyes at her comment. Kate lowered her eyes to avoid further discussion of her eating habits.

The waitress brought over the beers and walked away without saying anything to them. Kate looked around the room at the crowd. The majority of patrons consisted of bikers dressed in leather pants, leather vests, bandanas in their hair, and tattoos covering most of their skin. She looked down at her little black dress and felt completely embarrassed at how out-of-place she appeared. She was angry with Ben for bringing her to a place like this and not warning her to change clothes. *Why would he want to humiliate her like this?*

Ben smiled at her. "Cheer up! Okay, it's a bit of a dive and there's no anti-bacterial wipes on the tables, but they really do make great food. I promise you. Now, is it possible for you to relax and have a good time?" He held up his bottle of beer to clink a toast with her.

Kate was having a difficult time getting past all her annoying thoughts, but she refused to have him go back and tell Tom what a stick-in-the-mud she had been. She took a deep breath and straightened up in her seat. She picked up the bottle of beer, lightly tapped his, and forced herself to take a sip of it. The bitterness made her wince.

"I take it you don't drink beer much?" he asked.

"It's not my first choice, no." she said. Seeing his look of disappointment, she picked up the bottle again and took a big swallow, keeping her eyes on him the entire time. She set it down hard on the table. *I'm not a prude*, she thought to herself. She continued to stare at him, and he stared back. The contest was ended when the waitress came back to take their order.

Ben nodded to Kate for her to place her order first. "I'll have the salad," she told the waitress. Quickly, she darted her eyes to Ben, searching for a reaction. That look of disappointment came back to his face again, but her delicate stomach was stronger than her pride, and could not allow her to order anything else. Ever since she could remember, Kate had a very delicate constitution. Acid reflux was the latest term to describe it these days. No matter what the label, her body reacted horribly to spicy, hot foods. It was probably all connected to her tightly-wound nervous system, and deep down, she knew that. But rather than learning to confront her anxiety, fears, and stress, she chose to simply avoid anything that might agitate or irritate. She'd turned that approach into a way of life.

"I'll have the number five, number eighteen, number twenty-one, and an extra side order of rice," said Ben. He looked at Kate to read her reaction and turned back to the waitress. "And bring me another one of these, please," he said, tapping on his beer bottle.

Kate could feel the alcohol beginning to flow through her body, and it felt good after a very stressful past few days. Between the beer and her pain medication, her tension softened, and even Ben couldn't upset her anymore. She looked across the table at him working on his second beer. She examined his large, sad eyes, gazing about the restaurant. Was he hoping to catch the eye of a potential one-night-stand? It dawned on Kate at that moment that she had never seen Ben with a girlfriend. Obviously, she found him extremely repulsive, but certainly there existed women out there who found his type intriguing—perhaps even charming? She watched as Ben wrapped his wet, full lips around his bottle of beer. A drop of it slipped down his chin, and Ben quickly wiped the drip and turned to see if Kate had seen him. Sensing his embarrassment, Kate averted her eyes back to her own beer bottle, lifted it, and drank.

To avoid further conversation, she gazed around the restaurant. The dark, rough-hewn boards from ceiling to floor did not seem to appropriately express the ambience of an Indian restaurant. No, her guess was this had once been a seafood pub that had been purchased by a family of immigrants, who had no funds for remodeling. The air smelled of stale beer and old grease—most likely from twenty years of unwashed surfaces. She examined the wood chair rail next to her seat, adorned with bits of dried ketchup and cobwebs. Apparently, something was good here, because there wasn't an empty seat in the place on a Monday night. She watched, jealously, as the customers around her laughed and drank with such carefree pleasure. It felt as if the world was dancing all around her, while she slowly made her exit from it.

The waitress returned with three plates of food for Ben and a bowl of lettuce for her. "Wow!" said Ben. "This looks fantastic!" He looked over at her measly meal and said, "Feel free to try some of mine."

"Thank you, but no," Kate said politely, picking at her lettuce leaves.

Ben attacked his food with boundless energy—stabbing at number eighteen, gulping number five, and shoveling number twenty-one down with a large spoonful of rice. In between swallows, he would moan, "Mmmmmmmmmm—wow!" She slightly envied his enjoyment. She'd never experienced such joy over a meal.

Kate took some bites of her iceberg lettuce covered in a yogurt-cucumber dressing, and attempted to look pleased, by smiling at Ben while she chewed. It really was tolerable. How badly could you screw up lettuce, anyway?

"What a great day, huh?" said Ben, attempting to take the focus off of the food. "We had that guy, Jeff, eating out of our hands! You know, I could really get into this sales thing. It sure beats customer service."

"His name is Jack," said Kate. "If you want to be in sales, the first thing you need to do is remember people's names. And I wouldn't say he was eating out of our hands. I think we just have a superior product that came across in my—our—presentation." *God, he's so thoughtless! Does he ever think of anyone but himself? One successful sale and he's suddenly a salesman! I'm going to need more beer, if I'm ever going to get through this night.*

Kate picked up her bottle and held it there till it was empty. Then she shoved lettuce in her mouth as fast as she could. The sooner she finished, the closer she was to saying goodnight to this guy.

"Jack...yeah...whatever," said Ben, as he picked up his bottle and tossed back the last of his second beer. He suddenly looked pensive, as if he was contemplating her last remarks. Then a switch was thrown and he was back to himself. "How's that salad?" Before she could answer, he continued, "Hey, that's interesting. They put raisins in your salad. Must be some Indian thing."

16

Kate stopped eating and looked down at her nearly empty bowl. "That's not a raisin," she said. "It's a bug." She dropped her fork and pushed the bowl away from her. She wanted to throw up at that moment, but she fought the urge. Instead, her eyes filled with tears. Maybe it was the alcohol. Maybe it was her medication. Maybe it was Ben. Maybe it was the cockroach in the bottom of her salad. She didn't know anymore. She couldn't name exactly what it was that was causing her such grief. She just knew she'd had enough for the night. Tears flowed down her cheeks as she slid out of the booth and pushed past the crowds to the door.

Ben threw down some cash on the table and followed her out onto the sidewalk, where she was briskly walking toward their hotel. As he caught up to her, he said, "Do you need to throw up?"

"No," said Kate, calmly. "I just need to go to my room." There was nothing that could be done to make this night bearable for her, except to end it. She focused her thoughts on getting on the plane the next day and flying back to home—to Tom.

"Kate, I'm so sorry about the restaurant. Let me take you somewhere else," he said, grabbing her arm and hoping to make her stop walking away from him.

"No!" said Kate sharply. "I don't want anything else!" She pulled her arm away from Ben's grasp and turned around. But as she did, her three-inch heel dug into a crack in the sidewalk. *Snap!* She heard as it broke off from the rest of her shoe. She immediately looked down at her beautiful, barely-worn, and now broken, black sling-back pump.

A look of horror came over Ben's face as she lifted her gaze back to him. But she couldn't say anything more. Her face scrunched into twisted, troll-like knot. The tears welled up in her already-bloodshot eyes, but no sound could she make. Nor did she need to make a sound at that point that could more fully convey her thoughts of frustration to Ben at that moment. Ben reached down quickly and grabbed the heel from the cracked pavement and brought it up to Kate's face. Silently, she took the heel from his hand, twirled around, and began hobbling down the sidewalk toward their hotel. Ben followed her, keeping about three paces behind for safety, and neither spoke a word for the entire walk back to the rooms.

As soon as the door of her room was closed, Kate stripped her dress off and kicked her shoes across the room. She walked to the bathroom and ran cold water over her face, before scrubbing her teeth for an excessive amount of time. There was nothing she could do to stop the tears. The amount of stress that she had balanced so carefully in the last few days—perhaps from the last six months—had finally been toppled by a cockroach.

She fell asleep that night without calling Tom. Her phone battery and her own internal battery drained down to nothing while she slept.

Chapter 4

She woke up at four o'clock, showered, dressed and packed her suitcase. By five they were in a cab and on their way to LAX to catch their six-thirty flight to Atlanta.

At the airport Kate asked Ben to watch her bag while she went to the restroom. She despised using the restrooms on the plane. She found a ladies' room nearby and went in. She followed her standard routine of wiping the stall and the toilet seat down with her antibacterial wipes, and then placed the paper liner on top of the seat before settling down to pee.

As she exited the restroom she was nearly knocked down by several people running past her. The usual sounds of an airport terminal were gone and had been replaced with a spirit of anxiety. Everyone seemed to be on their cell phone, and almost everyone looked either scared or they were crying. She walked up to Ben from behind. "What's going on?" she asked.

Ben turned to face her. His mouth was open like he'd seen a ghost. "What?" she asked angrily.

"They just canceled our flight," he said almost as if he was in a daze.

"What?" she asked—completely perplexed. "What do you mean they canceled our flight? Why?"

"They canceled all flights," Ben said. "Someone just flew two airliners into the World Trade Center. They're not letting anybody board a plane."

Kate stood there in shock and disbelief. A chill ran up her neck as she tried to comprehend what he was saying. A nearby television caught her eye and she watched in horror as a plane disappeared into the second tower and turned glass and steel into smoke and ash. Her head was swimming with questions. *What was happening? Were we at war? What should we do? Was this real?*

Ben put his hands on her shoulders to gain her attention away from the TV. "There's no telling how long this shut down could last. We could be stuck here for days. Stay here and I'll see if I can find another way to get home," he said.

"Okay," Kate replied obediently. She took their bags and looked for the nearest wall she could lean against, while she waited for him to return. She noticed again now that everyone around her was on a cell phone. It occurred to her that she should call Tom and let him know that she was alright. She reached in her purse, pulled out her phone, and dialed his number.

"Kate! Are you okay? Are you in a plane?" Tom asked frantically.

"I'm fine, Tom," she said calmly. "I'm in the airport. Our flight never boarded. But all flights are canceled. Ben is trying to find us another way home right now."

"Okay. Good. You're in good hands with Ben," he said relieved. "You'll be fine. I'm just so glad you're safe."

"This is so crazy, Tom!" she said. "What is happening? Do they know who did this?" But there was only silence on the other end. The connection had failed and she had no bars on her phone. She threw the phone back in her purse angrily. Just then Ben came walking up quickly.

"I was able to rent a car. I think we better get it fast. If this situation escalates all hell could break loose and we'll be battling for our vehicle," he said firmly.

Kate looked into his eyes. She could see that he was deeply concerned about their safety. She picked up her bag and followed him to the parking lot. Halfway across the lot a young man bumped into

Kate and almost knocked her down. He was gone before she could even say, "He took my purse!"

"Forget it," said Ben. He continued to walk toward the car. "Let's just get in the car and get out of here!"

"Forget it?" she said fervently, as she followed him and attempted to pull him back. "Everything I own is in that bag! I can't just forget it! Please go after him! My phone, my money..." She tugged at him, hoping he would understand her urgency to retrieve the purse.

Once again, he took her forcibly by the shoulders to get her undivided attention. "Look, Kate, there's nothing in there that can't be replaced. Right now we've got to get on the road. Four airplanes have crashed already. I don't know what the hell's going on out there, but I'm not sticking around at this goddamn airport waiting to find out."

Kate scowled but then looked up at the sky to see what was above her head. She knew he was right. She also knew that her pain pills were in that bag, and she had a long way to go without them. But she really didn't have a choice at this point. She jumped into the passenger seat and slammed the door. Ben started the little Honda Civic and squealed out of the lot. He made his way through the traffic and onto the interstate. "Fuck," he said as he looked down at the gauge. "We've got a half a tank of gas." They both looked over at the gas station coming up. The place was overrun with cars. Lines were forming down the street. "We'll get some when we get out of town," he said. "We've got plenty to get us far from here."

Kate turned on the car radio to get some news. It was obvious that everyone was a little confused by what had happened. There was talk that we were at war—but with whom? As the reports kept coming in, the news was just more and more depressing.

Once they were out of the city it seemed like everything around them was a desert. There were no gas stations, no restaurants, and no options. They turned off the air conditioning to save on fuel, which made it that much more uncomfortable as they drove down a lonely two-lane highway. Kate leaned over to see the gauge. "I don't know why you didn't stop at that last station before we left town," she asked agitated.

"I didn't want to wait in those lines, but I guess I should have just done it." He glanced down at the gas gauge. "Damn, we need to find

21

something now," he said. The car slowed, sputtered and died just three minutes later, and they were stranded. They sat there in a pool of sweat mulling over their choices.

"You stay here," Ben started, "I'll walk to the next gas station."

"Are you kidding me?" Kate shouted. "I'm not staying here alone! I'm going with you." She looked around. There was nothing but dirt and cactus as far as she could see.

Ben knew she was right and reluctantly agreed. They took off down the quiet road in the blazing heat of the afternoon sun to find refuge. There wasn't a cloud in the sky to offer them relief. Kate started thinking she would eventually just pass out from lack of oxygen, but somehow she kept going. "I didn't think this day could get any stranger, but it did," she said.

Ben laughed. "Yeah, that's for sure. Feels like we're living inside a Twilight Zone episode," he said. He stopped for a moment. "Listen. Look," he said as he pointed up to the sky. "No planes." He looked down at Kate. Just for a moment Kate wondered—even hoped—if she truly was inside the Twilight Zone. The strange set of events that had occurred in the last seven days could certainly qualify. Disappointed, she brought herself back to the idea that this was unfortunately reality.

"Do you think we are at war, Ben? Who could have done this?"

"I don't know," said Ben out of breath from the walk. "I don't know, but I hate their fucking guts right now."

The wind blew the desert dust at them and it stuck to the sweat on their faces and arms. By the time they reached a small motel three miles down the road they looked as if they had crawled out of the earth. Ben spotted the motel office in the corner of the one-story building. It had definitely seen better days. The wood siding appeared as if at one time it might have been painted white. In fact, it was possible that in 1957 this place would have been considered "cute." However, now it barely looked as it was even open. Ben walked to the open doorway. Kate followed him cautiously, carefully observing all around her before taking the next step. Inside the office was a middle-aged Mexican woman sitting at the desk. The little black and white TV behind her was replaying footage of the buildings engulfed in clouds of smoke. She turned her attention to Ben and Kate as they approached the desk.

"May I help you?" she asked.

"Yeah," said Ben. "How far to the nearest gas station?"

The woman frowned then rolled her eyes upward as she considered his question. "There's one about fifteen miles from here...if they've still got gas."

Ben looked around. "Any chance there's someone here who could drive us there?"

The woman said, "My husband, Jesse, can take you." Ben's face lit up but then quickly dropped as she continued, "He'll be here in the morning."

Ben turned around quickly so he could silently mutter, "Fuck!" Then he turned back around and smiled at the woman. "Anyone else nearby that we could get to help us? See, we ran out of gas about three miles back and we're trying to get to Atlanta."

"Yeah, I understand," said the woman sympathetically. "No, there's no one else around tonight. But Jesse will be here first thing in the morning and then he can take you." She smiled. She looked at Kate who had disappointment written all over her dusty face. "We have a vacancy. You can stay here tonight and then Jesse can take you in the morning!" she said optimistically.

Ben and Kate looked around at the office. They looked out the window at the empty parking lot. Obviously there was a vacancy. There had probably been a vacancy for the last twenty years from the looks of the place. Ben looked at Kate. She had a horrible frown on her face, which was common when she was looking at him. He sighed. "Okay, we'll stay. How much for the rooms?" he asked.

The woman looked overjoyed to have some customers. "Only forty dollars!" she said.

"Okay," said Ben as he pulled out a credit card from his wallet. "We'll take two rooms. Put them both on this card."

"Oh, we don't take credit cards here, sir," she said. "Only cash."

Ben sighed again and held his profanities inside while he dug through his wallet. "Okay. I've got thirty-five dollars. What do you say you cut us a break, given the circumstances?"

The woman looked disappointed but then put a smile on her face and said, "Okay. I give you a break."

"Great!" Ben said, and he handed her the cash.

The woman reached behind her and gave Ben a key.

"Uh, no, we need two rooms," he said to her.

"You only give me thirty-five dollars. I'm giving you a deal, mister. You get one room for thirty-five dollars."

At this point Ben was about to explode. He looked over at Kate. "I had money in my wallet," she said. "But somebody stole my purse this morning," she continued irritably.

Ben took the key from the woman and thanked her. "Let me know as soon as Jesse gets here in the morning!" he said to her.

"Sure thing!" she said and turned back to her television.

Ben and Kate walked down the sidewalk to their room in silence. They opened the door to find a dark wood-paneled room with green shag carpet. Ben flipped on the light switch to reveal one full size bed covered by a quilted floral bedspread. Kate looked around the room, then at the bed, and finally over at Ben. Ben looked down at her. "It's one night for God's sake," he said in response to her disapproving facial expression.

Kate headed to the bathroom without a word. She knew there was nothing she could say that could further express her disappointment and anger at the situation more than her face was already doing. Truth be told, she really didn't care too much at this point. She was hot, tired and hungry. She had no purse, no driver's license, no credit cards, no money, no antibacterial wipes, and no pain medication. She had a few weeks to live and she wasn't sure at this point if the world would end before she would. She closed the bathroom door and disrobed to take a shower. She carefully hung her clothes on the hook on the door. There wasn't a clean surface in sight. With two fingers, she carefully pulled back the shower curtain and turned the knob. She stepped out of her sandals one at a time to avoid putting her bare feet directly on the floor and gingerly stepped into the tub.

The water felt good on her sweaty face and neck as she stood under the weak spray from the shower head. She let it run over her entire body saturating her hair as well. She pulled the paper from the tiny bar of soap and did her best to work up a couple of suds to run across her skin. She closed her eyes, and visions of those two buildings crumbling were all that she could see. She quietly prayed to a God she didn't believe in that they were trapped in the Twilight Zone and she would wake in the morning to find it had all ended. It was all too surreal to grasp.

After she was dried off, there was no other option but to put her dirty clothes back on. She shook the dust from each article, dressed, and walked out of the bathroom. Ben was sitting on one side of the bed watching TV, eating Cheetos, and feeding the massage unit quarters. He was in the middle of a very loud belch, when he realized she was standing there watching him. "Hey," he said. "Feel better?" When she didn't reply, but only stared at him, he nervously looked around. Becoming aware that he was lying on the bed which she most likely intended for herself, he jumped to his feet.

"Oh, hey, sorry," he said smoothing out the bedspread with his cheese-powdered hands. He walked over to a chair in the corner, sat down and placed his feet on the table in front of him. "Lucky for us there was a vending machine outside that still worked. I know you don't drink soda so I got you a bottle of water and some cheese crackers. It was the healthiest thing I could find." He nodded to the items laying on the nightstand by the bed. Kate glanced over at them and mustered up a polite thank you, and Ben went back to watching television.

She carefully pulled back the sticky, grungy bedspread until it met the end of the bed and lay down on top of the sheets. An old "I Love Lucy" episode was on. She opened her bottle of water and started to watch the show. Anything other than reality was inviting right now.

"This is the one where Lucy tries to fool the kids at Little Ricky's birthday party into thinking she's Superman," said Ben. He laughed as he watched Lucy climb around on the outside of an apartment building wearing a helmet and a cape. Kate remembered this episode. She had grown up watching reruns. Soon they were both laughing hysterically at the show. Oh, how good it felt to laugh!

Just then Ben's cell phone rang. He picked it up and answered, "Hey buddy! What's up?" Silence followed as he listened to the caller. Then he proceeded, "Oh yeah...well, we had some setbacks. Yeah, she's fine....well...the car ran out of gas, so we had to walk till we found a motel... I don't know... Bum-fucked God-knows-where...yeah that's probably because some jackoff stole her purse..."

Kate realized he was talking to Tom and reached over for him to hand her the phone, but Ben ignored her and kept on talking. "Yeah," Ben continued. "I mean what the fuck, huh? Assholes are flying planes into buildings and the next thing you know someone's fucking mugging you in broad daylight. What the hell happened anyway? Do they know?" Ben asked.

Kate was getting really impatient. She got out of bed and stood next to Ben. "Let me talk to him," she whispered harshly.

Ben looked up at her. "Oh…yeah…hey Tom…Kate wants to talk to you…yeah she's right here…we only had enough money for one room…"

With that Kate ripped the phone out of Ben's hand. "Tom!" she said fiercely. "Tom, I'm sorry I couldn't call. My purse was stolen this morning and then we ran out of gas and we've been walking…"

"Ben said you're at a motel?" said Tom.

"Yes, we're staying in some God awful place off the interstate, and we're…"

"And you're sharing a room?" Tom asked slowly.

"Yes…there's only one bed…Ben's sleeping in a chair…Tom?" Kate asked when she could no longer hear him on the line. She pulled the phone away from her ear and looked at the screen. It was black. She rolled the phone around in her hand, pushing buttons trying to make the screen light up again but to no avail.

"Battery's dead," said Ben as he threw another handful of Cheetos into his mouth and continued to stare at the television.

"Great! Just great!" said Kate as she threw herself back onto the bed. Suddenly thinking she had a bright idea, she rolled over on the bed to the night stand on the opposite side and picked up the handset of the hotel phone. She triumphantly dialed "O" for the operator to make a collect call, but all she received was a recorded message telling her that all circuits were busy. Slamming the phone back into its cradle, Kate jumped out of the bed and began pacing around the room. "Damn it! Can't anything go right?" she screamed.

"Kate! Calm down already," said Ben from his chair. "Tom knows we're alright. Tomorrow we'll have a cell phone charger and a car…and gas. We'll call him tomorrow and everything will be fine." Again, he crunched down a mouthful of cheese puffs.

She looked desperately around the room for items to throw. "Calm down? Calm down? They make me go on this stupid trip. The next thing I know the world is ending! My *life* is ending, and I'm spending my last days on Earth with the person I hate most in this world! Jesus! How could it possibly get any worse? And you want me to calm down?" she shouted. She spun around to glare at him for his terribly inappropriate comment. But looking into Ben's sad, questioning eyes was all she needed to melt her hostility into shameful remorse for her words. She'd said it out loud. She'd said the most terrible thing to Ben out loud and there was no way of taking it back. He was still sitting in the chair and staring straight at her with a wounded look on his face. He looked into her eyes and then lowered his chin to stare at his lap.

"Wow," he said with a little hint of laughter. He raised himself up and leaned back in his chair. Hooking an elbow over the top of the chair, he said, "I had no idea I held that kind of honor with you. I mean to be the person someone hates the most…well…that's gotta be a pretty big deal."

Kate walked over to the bed and sat down with her back to him. "Hate was probably not the right word. I should have said…"

"You should have said what?" asked Ben. "Tell me, Kate, how do you rephrase what you just said to sound kinder and gentler?"

Kate sat in silence. She had no words to change what she had blurted out in anger. She saw no way to hide how she really felt, even though she felt horrible for saying it. She had hurt him, deeply, and for that she was truly sorry. "Ben, I'm just so mad," was all she could muster.

Ben stood up and walked to the door. "I guess we're all a little mad right now." He opened the door and walked through it without looking back at her. It slammed shut as he made his way out into the darkness.

Kate sat there in shock staring at the door. She felt really sick, and it wasn't from the cancer. She crawled back over to her pillow and hugged it tightly. Another episode of "I Love Lucy" was beginning and she settled into watching it to take her mind away from all the reality going on around her. But as hard as she tried, she could not focus on the episode. Her words and Ben's face just kept playing over and over in her head. "What a mark I am leaving on this world," she said in self-disgust.

Chapter 5

A loud pounding on the hotel room door woke Kate up out of a dead sleep. She raised her head up to see Ben asleep in the chair by the table. He must have crept back into the room after she fell asleep, and she had never heard him. She raised her head up and whispered as loud as she could, "Ben! Ben! There's someone at the door!"

Ben was startled by her and shook his head to try and wake himself. The pounding on the door began again and he jumped up out of the chair. He flipped on the light switch and opened the door to find a large Mexican man in his late fifties standing there. "You need someone to drive you to the gas station?" he asked.

"Uh, yeah...yeah," Ben said as he rubbed his eyes. He turned around to look at Kate. "You ready?"

"Yes!" said Kate as she jumped out of the bed and drug her fingers through her tousled hair.

They followed the man out to the parking lot and climbed into the cab of his rusty, old, red pick-up truck. The cold fresh air hit them in the face like a slap to wake them out of their sleepy state. It was four-

29

thirty, and the sun was not up yet. The man started the noisy engine and said, "My name is Jesse."

Ben said, "I'm Ben and this is Kate. We really appreciate you helping us out."

"No problem," said Jesse as he pulled out of the parking lot and onto the service road.

The three rode in sleepy silence to the gas station. Ben filled up a can full of gas and then Jesse took them back to their car on the interstate. Ben tried to give Jesse some money that he'd pulled from his credit card at the station, but he refused to take it. "Just take care, okay?" said Jesse.

Ben shook Jesse's hand and patted him on the shoulder. "Yeah man, you too, Jesse. Thanks big time."

Kate felt a sense of relief come over her as they pulled back out onto the highway in their little rental car to head home. Ben was quiet. She sensed he had not forgiven her for what she had said the night before. She thought it was probably best if she didn't say anything more, so she sat in silence as the sun began to light up a pink sky on the horizon in front of them.

"You hungry?" Ben asked a few miles down the road.

Kate sighed. "Yes, I am."

Ben took the next exit and landed the car in the parking lot of a McDonald's. "I'm pretty sure there is nothing they serve here that you like, but this is where we're eating. Like it or not. I don't care," he said in an exhausted voice. They both got out of the car and walked into the restaurant. Ben walked up to the counter and began ordering. "I'll take two sausage biscuits, a large OJ, an order of hash browns, and a large coffee." Then he turned around to Kate. "Go ahead and tell him what you want."

Kate looked a little stunned. She hadn't eaten in a fast food restaurant in years. She squinted up at the brightly lit menu above her head contemplating what would be healthy. She sensed the anxiety of the person waiting to take her order which was only matched by the impatience of the line of people behind her. "Um...I'll take a large coffee," she could feel all the eyes upon her and it made her nervous to know she was pissing off so many people. "And hotcakes and sausage. Do you have turkey sausage?" she asked. The guy at the counter looked at her like she was from another planet. She felt the people behind her moan with grief. "Never mind, I'll just take hotcakes and sausage. That's all...and the coffee." She quickly got out of line while Ben handed over his credit card to pay. Afraid to meet the stares of anyone in line behind her, Kate kept her head down as she found her way to the ladies' room.

Kate looked at herself in the bathroom mirror. Her hair was a mess, but she had no comb to fix it, so she ran her fingers through it to get it to lay flat. She leaned in closer to examine her eyes. Dark circles were starting to form under them. Just then a pain went through her stomach like a knife. She gasped at the suddenness of it. Then she closed her eyes and worked to take deep breaths and force herself to relax. She was going to have to get some pain medication soon. She gave herself one more glance in the mirror and then walked out.

Ben was seated at a table with both of their trays already there. He was busy chomping away at his sausage biscuit and pouring ketchup all over his hash browns. Kate sat down opposite him and began eating her hotcakes. She pulled the piece of breakfast sausage out from under the cakes with her fork. "Do you want this?" she asked Ben. Ben reached out with his fingers and grabbed it off of her fork. She wasn't sure if he was just famished or if he was still giving her the silent treatment from her comments last night. She decided to concentrate on eating her breakfast so they could get back on the road.

Ben crammed a half of a sausage biscuit into his mouth. "We better hurry if we're going to make any progress today," he said as biscuit crumbs flew out of his over-crowded mouth. Kate just stared in disbelief that this person could possibly be Tom's best friend. Ben wiped his mouth with the back of his hand and stood up to indicate he was ready to go.

Ben pulled into a gas station to fill the tank full and purchase a map. Kate searched the aisles of the quick shop for a comb, toothbrush, toothpaste and some Tylenol. "I'll pay you back," Kate said at the counter as Ben swiped his credit card for all their things.

"No big deal," he said as he headed out the door for the car.

Ben jumped back into the car. He studied the map for a few minutes and then tossed it into the back seat without folding it. He leaned forward, cranked up some AC/DC playing on the radio, and peeled out of the gas station lot. Kate was starting to feel drowsy after her breakfast and a couple of Tylenol she'd taken for her pain. She tried desperately to fight the temptation to nod off, but soon there was nothing she could do about it but give in. Besides, it was obvious that Ben was not interested in conversing with her.

Chapter 6

She didn't even realize she'd fallen asleep until the vehicle suddenly took a screeching turn up an exit ramp. Her head thumped against the glass of the passenger window as the car struggled to get back on an even course. Confused and frightened she screamed, "What are you doing?"

Ben was calm as always. "Boy, you sure sleep a lot. Have you ever seen the Painted Desert?" he asked Kate.

"No," she replied.

"Me neither," he said. "But it's right here and I want to see it, so we're going." He turned off the overpass onto a little road that wound its way to the entry gates into the desert.

Kate felt her anger rising up, but she decided it would be better if she remained silent. Instead, she sat there staring straight ahead quietly fuming. It was difficult enough making this trip with him and now it was turning into a vacation—a vacation from hell. They drove on for what seemed like miles without seeing anything but dirt. The thought of wasting precious time was getting to her and she just had to speak up. "Are you sure this is it? I don't see anything but rocks."

Ben shook his head but stared straight ahead. He followed the two lane highway through the desolate terrain until they arrived at the first scenic overlook. He stopped the car and jumped out almost immediately. Kate sat there trying to decide if she wanted to stay mad or get out and look. After a few moments, curiosity won out, and she opened the door. The intense wind smacked her in the face as she stepped out of the car. She pushed her hair out of her eyes and headed up the hill to see what was holding Ben's fascination.

By the time she reached the top of the hill she could no longer hold on to her anger. The sight before her was too breathtaking to ignore and her negative feelings melted quickly. In front of her lay an immense field of boulders, crushed rock, and desert blooms. The afternoon sun danced across pale stones, painting them gold on a canvas of burnt orange, soft tans, and gentle brushstrokes of sage green. She stood there simply amazed by this wonder of nature, when Ben finally spoke. "Fucking awesome, huh?"

"Yes," she said. "It really does look like a painting. The colors are incredible."

"Let's keep walking down this path," said Ben with his hands on her shoulders coaxing her along. "I want to walk for a while."

Kate obediently walked along with him looking out at the basin as she did so. They finally came to a place that satisfied Ben enough to stay. They both leaned forward on the railing side by side. The wind blew fiercely, but there was hardly a sound. Tears formed in her eyes. She wasn't sure if it was from the wind or the sheer beauty she was witnessing. "It's so peaceful here—such a contrast to what's going on right now," said Kate.

"Yeah, you're right," said Ben. "We're lucky."

"Why do you think they did it?" she asked. Ben looked at her confused. "The planes, I mean…why did it happen?"

"Because the bastards hate us, that's why. They hate us because we live and breathe and it just repulses them to know we exist." He let a few seconds go by before he added, "Kinda like how you feel about me."

Kate whirled around to look at him on that comment. She wasn't sure what she was going to say, because she knew she had it coming. What she saw was Ben's ever familiar smirk which told her he was enjoying this moment way too much, and he had forgiven her. She took a deep breath, erased the look of anger from her face and replaced it with a kind smile.

"Ben, I'm sorry. I was angry last night, but that's still no excuse for what I said." She turned to look out over the desert, so she wouldn't have to meet his gaze. "It's very obvious that you and I are very different—complete opposites in fact. There are times... well; most times...I find your behavior to be irritating..."

"Kate!" Ben interrupted, "Please don't spoil this moment."

Kate took the hint and stopped talking. They walked on a little further until they came to some large boulders. They both sat down and looked around them as the angle of the sun continued to lengthen and create an entirely new palette before their eyes. Ben broke the silence. "I know you said last night that your life was about to end, but this isn't the end, Kate. We'll fight back on this terrorist thing and we'll win. You'll be alright. You'll see."

Kate continued looking straight ahead. She half-smiled realizing that Ben had no idea what she had meant last night. She wrestled with the idea of telling him the truth. She hadn't even told Tom yet, but now Tom was thousands of miles away and she had no one else in which to confide. She wanted so badly to tell him, yet she was afraid to hear it said out loud. *Would saying it make it more real?* Up until now it had felt like a dream. *Would not saying it make it go away?* Quietly she cleared her throat and said quickly before she could change her mind, "Ben, I'm dying." She darted her eyes quickly to his face to catch his expression and then moved them back onto the scene in front of her. *There, I've made it real*, she thought to herself.

Ben turned to look at her. "What? What are you talking about?"

Kate turned to look at Ben. The sun caught her eyes and she threw her hand over them so she could see his reaction. "I'm dying. It's cancer. I found out on Friday. I just haven't told anybody yet...until now."

Ben just kept looking at her, searching her eyes for the truth. "You're serious, aren't you?" he finally said.

"Dead serious—ooh—poor choice of words I guess. Yes, it's really going to happen," she said.

Ben stood up and walked a few feet in front of her with his hands on top of his head as if he were trying to stop what he was hearing. He turned around to face her and his hands dropped to his side. "Does

Tom know?" he asked. "Oh, that's right. You just said you haven't told him yet. Geez! I don't know what else to say!"

She looked down at her hands where her fingers were nervously picking at each other. "I should have told him before I went on this trip, but I hated to leave him holding that kind of information in his head until I returned."

Ben wiped his hand over his face and then began walking towards her. He knelt down in front of her. "Are you sure? I mean…are you sure? They make mistakes all the time."

"I'm sure," she said. "I've been having tests and x-rays done all year. My doctor's had other specialists look at the results, and it's just not going away."

He jumped back up and began pacing. "Shit," he said.

Kate looked up at him. "Yep, it's shit alright."

"Why aren't you crying? I'd be bawling my eyes out right now if I were you. You've been holding this in since Friday? How can you be so calm about it?"

Kate laughed at the irony of his question. She didn't think she'd been calm at all. Didn't he just tell her last night to calm down? "I don't know," she said. "I thought when I told you just now that it would make me cry, but I just can't. I mean… I have cried about it." She stood up from the boulder and said, "We should get going. It's going to be dark soon." The two of them started back for the car.

After she'd buckled herself in, she looked over at Ben and said, "Thank you for bringing me here. It's the most beautiful place I've ever seen. I'll never forget it." Tears began to trickle from her eyes and she looked away from him in embarrassment.

"I'm glad you got to see it," said Ben.

She put her hand on his arm and said, "I'm sorry about last night. It was a horrible thing to say."

"But you spoke the truth. You meant it."

"I suppose I meant it at the time—in a fit of anger and frustration. I'm a perfectionist, Ben. I've always expected everything to be perfect, neat and tidy. I expected you to fit into that as well, but you didn't, so it made me mad." Tears filled her eyes again and were soon spilling over her face. "Nothing in my life is perfect anymore! Nothing is going according to the plans that I had! Nothing is neat and clean! I'm completely out of control!" She wiped her eyes and began searching for a tissue to catch her dripping nose. Giving up on the search, she dragged her hand across the bottom of her nose. She laughed at herself. "See? I'm a snotty mess!" She looked out the window and continued, "I always wanted to die like Barbara Hershey did in the movie *Beaches*. You know—lying in a lounge chair next to the ocean, watching the sunset, and just fading away with the sun. Instead I'm sitting in a car driving across country—looking more like Jon Voight in *Midnight Cowboy*."

"Um, I think that was Dustin Hoffman. Jon Voight was the prostitute," Ben said quietly.

"Whatever," said Kate. They both laughed.

"Kate, you're not going to die in the car! We're going to be home in a couple of days." Ben said. But then he got quiet. "How long do you have?"

"The doctor doesn't seem to know for sure, but he said it could be weeks…maybe."

Ben's eyes were glistening with tears. He looked away from her and wiped them with his hand. He leaned over to her so he could look into her eyes and said, "Listen, I'm going to get you home as fast as I can. Okay? You're not going to die on the road. You've had a fuckin' shitty last few days, but that's about to change. We're going to get you a good dinner and then we're going to drive. I can at least get us into Oklahoma. Then we'll stay in a real hotel with clean sheets and hot water. Next day—we're in Atlanta. Okay?"

"Okay," said Kate as she sniffled. Her tears had nearly all dried up while he spoke to her. She sat there wide-eyed, watching him with a new-found respect for his character. She smiled at him to show that she was really accepting what he said as truth. Relieved that she believed him, he leaned back over to the steering wheel, turned the ignition on, and put the car in gear. A few hours down the road, they stopped at a restaurant of Kate's choice and then quickly slipped back onto the interstate, heading for Oklahoma.

Kate woke up with her head against the passenger window. They were in a parking lot of a Best Western hotel. Just then she saw Ben at her door. She sat up and pulled up on the lock. "We're here," he said.

"Where?" she asked sleepily, wiping the drool from her cheek.

"Oklahoma," said Ben. He held out his hand to help Kate out of the car. She graciously accepted his hand. "Sorry. It's not the Hilton, but at least it's clean."

"A real hotel tonight...ahhh... I can't wait to take a shower and wash my hair."

"Yeah, I can't wait either. You smell like shit. I didn't want to say anything to make you feel bad."

"Oh, stop it!" she said, realizing he was just teasing her.

She figured she must have been sleeping for several hours. The last thing she remembered was leaving a steakhouse in New Mexico. After dinner, she called Tom on Ben's recharged cell phone to tell him they were alright. She explained the confusion of the night before and told him they would be home soon. She felt a little guilty as she hung up the phone. Not only had she kept her secret from Tom, but she had shared it with Ben. It felt wrong, but she would make it right when she was back in Atlanta.

Safe inside her hotel room, she took a long, hot shower. She massaged shampoo and conditioner into her hair for several minutes, delighting in the feeling of being clean and fragranced again. After her shower, she slipped into bed and turned on the TV. She thought about calling Tom collect, but she just wasn't in the mood to talk anymore. She changed the channel from the loop of the burning twin towers to another "I Love Lucy" rerun. The phone rang and she picked it up expecting to hear Tom, but to her surprise, it was Ben's voice on the line. "You okay?" he asked. "You need me to bring you anything?"

The sound of his voice on the other end made her feel surprisingly relieved. She happily replied, "No, I'm fine. I'm in bed watching *Lucy*."

"Me too!" he said laughing. "Okay, well I just thought I'd check."

"Ben," said Kate quietly. "Thanks for listening to me today."

"Hey, no problem, I just wish there was something I could do."

"Yeah," she said sadly, "me, too." She tried to think of something else to say to keep him on the line, but her mind was blank. For some strange reason, she didn't want to let him go. For a split second she thought about asking him to come over to watch TV with her, but the social awkwardness of it all made her change her mind. After a minute or two of silence, she reluctantly said, "Well, goodnight."

"Goodnight," said Ben.

She listened until she heard the familiar click and the dial tone. The horrible beeping sound forced her to move the handset away from her ear, but she continued to hold it in her hands. She looked down at it rethinking their short conversation—wishing she could have been craftier to keep him talking longer. Now she couldn't sleep. *Should she call him back and tell him she couldn't sleep? They could comment on the Lucy episode! No...just go to sleep and relax knowing he's just in the room next door. Let that be enough for tonight.* She put the handset back in its cradle and sunk down into her pillows. Before the episode was over, she was fast asleep.

Chapter 7

She woke up at six o'clock, forgetting that she'd lost an hour and scrambled to get ready for the road. Ben knocked on her door at six-thirty, and she was just zipping up her suitcase. They grabbed some coffee and a donut in the lobby and were on their way again by five minutes to seven.

Things seemed fresher today to Kate. She wasn't exactly sure why, but she felt more optimistic. Maybe it was because she was getting closer to home. Maybe it was because of the talk she had with Ben the day before. Maybe it was just because she had slept in a real bed. Regardless of why, she was just glad of the feeling. Ben seemed like he was in a good mood also.

"Hey," he said. "You know where I'm going to take you today?"

Kate shrugged her shoulders as he looked over at her.

"We're going through Memphis, and we are going to get you the best ribs you've ever had!"

"Ribs?" asked Kate in her usual arrogant style. "I don't eat ribs." As soon as she said it, she regretted it. *There you go, sounding like a snob again.*

"Well, today you are," said Ben firmly. He looked straight ahead at the road and smiled. "I know a great place and you're gonna love 'em!"

"Is it a really *nice* place like the one you took me to in Marina Del Ray?" Kate asked sarcastically.

Ben ignored her comment. "We're going to eat ribs slathered in barbecue sauce, greasy French fries, coleslaw, and wash it all down with some ice cold beer."

Kate slid down in her seat and stretched out her legs. She could tell there was no fighting him on this, so she might as well relax and wait for the "ribfest" to begin. Deep down, she sensed her own excitement at the thought of an adventure.

They arrived in Memphis in the early afternoon. Ben parked and led Kate down the sidewalk to the famous Beale Street. The street was heavily crowded with men and women walking up and down enjoying beer and other beverages that they held in huge cups. Acrobats were doing flip-flops down the center of the street, and vendors peddled their wares next to souvenir shops.

Ben pulled Kate into a large restaurant called BB King's Blues Club. They were seated upstairs overlooking the stage which was set up for a band to start at any minute. The waitress came by and Ben ordered a beer. Kate ordered an iced tea. She looked over the menu of barbecued meats and sides, but was reluctant to try any of them. Barbecue was messy and sticky. As curious as she was about tasting it, she was not accustomed to wearing her food. No, it was much smarter to stick with a green salad. When the waitress came back for their order Ben said, "Give me the full slab of ribs, fries and baked beans."

The waitress looked over at Kate. She closed her menu, set it down, and said, "I'll have the salad."

"No, she won't!" said Ben. Kate glared at him across the brightly painted table. He looked up at the waitress. "She'll have the ribs and chicken plate and fries. Thanks." The waitress scribbled the order on the note pad and walked away.

"Ben!" Kate said firmly. "I don't eat this kind of food! I have a very delicate stomach and I have to be very careful what I eat."

"Seriously?" asked Ben. "Kate, people eat this food every day. Babies eat this stuff. Old people without teeth eat it. You're trying to tell me that a thirty-nine-year-old, healthy—reasonably healthy although somewhat dying—can't stomach some simple barbecued meat? Give me a break, woman. Do me a favor—just once. Eat the barbecue!" His intensity left Kate speechless, so he continued. "If you have to throw up later, you can do it in the car, I don't care. It's a rental." He winked at her and turned to look at the band that was just warming up.

Kate sat back and listened to the music. She was a little frustrated by Ben's aggression, but she was also tired and didn't feel much like fighting him anymore. When she saw how great her food looked she had to admit at least to herself that she wanted to try it. She picked up a fork and proceeded to tear a piece of meat from the rib. The sweet, smoky, tender meat melted in her mouth, and in the manner of a child, she delightedly exclaimed, "Mmm!"

"See! I told you so!" said Ben. It's the best. Now, just one more thing—put down that fork and pick up the rib like a human! Rip the meat off with your teeth. See? It falls right off the bone," he said as he pulled a hunk of meat off and dripped sauce down his chin.

The band was playing traditional blues music, and Kate began to relax a little, enjoy the music—and the food. Ben ordered two more beers and convinced her to drink one. It really did taste better with barbecue than iced tea did. By the time she was finished eating, she was covered in sauce as much as Ben was. She laughed at herself as she examined her sticky fingers and tried her best to lick it off her chin with her tongue. Ben smiled and laughed as he watched her finally having some fun.

"We got a dance floor down here, ya'll! Let's use it!" yelled the lead singer of the band.

Ben nodded to Kate. "C'mon. Let's go dance."

Kate stopped smiling and looked frightened. "No! Absolutely not!" she commanded.

"C'mon," Ben said standing up and taking her hand. She fought him for a while, but then he looked at her and said, "What are you afraid of?"

It could have been the beer, but Ben's question came at her hard like a dare direct from the devil. What did she have to be afraid of at this point? Certainly not making a fool of herself on the dance floor, so she rose to her feet. He led her out into the middle of the crowd already spinning and twirling, to 'Brown-eyed Girl'. Ben was a much better dancer than she ever imagined—not that she had ever imagined Ben dancing. Furthermore, she never imagined—in her wildest dreams—that *she* would be dancing with Ben! She had definitely had too much alcohol. She was losing control. Ben put her into a twirl, but just then a serious pain shot through her, and she grabbed her side.

Ben put his arms around her. "You okay? Is it the barbecue?"

"No," said Kate, without looking up. "I think we better go though."

Ben paid the check and helped her to the car as quickly as he could. When they were back inside the car he said, "You sure you're okay? Should I take you to a hospital?"

"No," she said still wincing in pain. "It will pass." She looked out the window as they drove away from the city. She took deep breaths and laid back in her seat until the pain subsided.

"Didn't the doctor give you anything for the pain?" Ben asked.

"Yes. He did. I had it in my purse, which was stolen," said Kate with a frown.

Ben slapped his face with his hand. "Oh God, Kate! I didn't know. Damn! I should've run after that guy!"

"It's too late now," she said. "Let's just forget about it." She tried to find a comfortable position in the car seat.

Suddenly Ben said, "Kate, can't you call your doctor and get him to call out a prescription for you? You know, I hear there's one on every corner."

She looked over at Ben in amazement. Why hadn't she thought of that? "Give me your phone," she said with a smile.

Within an hour, she had a prescription picked up from the nearest Walgreens, and they were on the road to Atlanta. Feeling "normal" again, Kate closed her eyes and fell asleep while Ben drove them quickly back home.

Chapter 8

They pulled into town around midnight. Stopped in her driveway, Ben looked over at her. She was staring at the light on in the living room. She could see Tom through the curtain watching television. She looked over at Ben. Before she could even say it, he said, "I won't say anything." Goosebumps went down her arm. She smiled at him in appreciation. Then he got out of the car and carried her suitcase to the door for her. Kate rang the doorbell, and Tom answered it with a look of excitement and relief to see her.

Tom grabbed her in his arms and held her tightly. "Babe! God, I missed you!" He looked at Ben standing there holding her suitcase. "Thanks for bringing her home safely, man."

"No problem," said Ben. He followed them into the house and set her suitcase down. "Well, I better get going. Back to work tomorrow."

Kate walked him to the door. "Thanks for everything Ben," she said smiling sincerely at him.

Ben smiled at her but said nothing. He just turned and walked out the door to the car. Kate watched him drive away and then closed the door. For the first time in her life, she felt sad to see Ben leave. Maybe the feeling was more about what was coming next. She dreaded the conversation she still had to have with Tom. The pains were coming more often. She was going to have to tell him quickly.

She locked the door and turned around to see Tom standing in the middle of the room looking at her. She rushed over to him and put her arms around his neck. "I missed you so much!" she said as she buried her face in his shirt.

Tom stroked her back with his hands and said, "I missed you too, babe. Man, what a horrible ordeal! You must be exhausted. Why don't we get ready for bed and you can tell me all the details."

"That's a great idea, Tom. I think I'm going to take a long, hot bath."

"Right!" he said. "I'll pour us some wine and bring it to you."

Kate looked back at him as she started for the bathroom. "How did I get so lucky?"

Tom laughed at her. "I'll be right in," he said.

She lay there in the hot sudsy water and thought back over the last few days. It had certainly been an adventure from the moment they got to the airport. *My purse!* She suddenly remembered. *I've got to cancel all my credit cards. Get a new cell phone. Insurance cards...oh...call the doctor...* Tom walked in the room just then and broke her thoughts. He handed her a glass of chardonnay and sat on the toilet.

"So, how was Ben? I mean, I know that he tends to get on your nerves. Did you get along okay?" he asked.

Kate thought for a moment. "It went surprisingly well actually."

"Really?" said Tom. "Wow! I kind of thought you'd be ready to kill him by now."

Kate smiled at his comment. "We got off on a rough start, but then things sort of worked themselves out." She took a sip of her wine. "Mmmm....tastes good," she said. She was somewhat hoping the subject would change. She wasn't in the mood to tell him all the details of her trip just now.

"Other than a terrorist attack, did anything exciting happen?" Tom asked curiously.

"I saw the Painted Desert," she volunteered.

"Hey, that's great. I've never seen it. At least something good came out of all this, huh? Hey, what is that in your hair?" he asked as he reached over to touch the strands just next to her face. "It kind of looks like... barbecue sauce."

"Oh!" said Kate. She grabbed the hair and began wiping it with her wet fingers. "Yeah, Ben took me to this great barbecue place in Memphis for lunch today."

"Barbecue? I didn't think you liked barbecue. Sounds like you two had a pretty good time—the Painted Desert, barbecue...," said Tom.

She looked at him sensing a teeny bit of jealousy. "Ben did his best to make the most of a really difficult situation, Tom."

"Oh...yeah...of course," Tom said realizing his state of mind might be showing. "That's good. Ben's good at that."

"I feel a little bit guilty— having enjoyed myself so much while all those people died and their families are suffering through this whole thing," she said.

"Yeah," said Tom. "But it's just these kinds of moments that make you realize that life is short and you've got to live it to the fullest while you still can. Don't knock yourself too much. You were just doing what you were supposed to do with your life."

Kate could feel her face turn red. "And what's that?" she asked.

"Enjoy it." He returned. Tom smiled at her and took a long sip of wine.

She lifted her glass and took a big swallow of chardonnay. Looking straight ahead at her toes sticking up through the suds, she said, "You're right, Tom. We've got to live while we still can."

She decided that evening was not the right time to tell him. It was getting late, and then they would be up all night discussing her illness. Tomorrow was Friday, and she had the whole weekend to tell him. Plus she would see the doctor tomorrow and maybe have more details.

She snuggled under Tom's shoulder as they lay in her bed. It was good to be home. She fell asleep remembering how it felt to be standing in the middle of the desert, listening to the wind rush through the valleys, and immersed in the splendor of the natural beauty of the earth.

Chapter 9

As soon as Tom left in the morning Kate called her doctor to make an appointment and get some new meds called out to her pharmacy. While they were on the road, he had only prescribed a few to get her back home. When she arrived at work the first person she saw was Ben. He was sitting on his desk while half a dozen employees stood around listening to the story of his cross-country road trip. As Kate passed by he stopped his storytelling to say, "Hey." Kate nodded to him as she would have any other day before their trip had taken place and slipped into her office. Realizing she was not going to engage him this morning, he went back to his captive audience. She blushed, hoping desperately that he wouldn't say anything about her to their coworkers. Surely he understood the importance of keeping her story private. She felt like they had developed a good rapport during their days together, but could she count on that to continue now that they were back at home?

A few minutes later Ben popped his head in her door. "Hey, how'd it go last night?"

"I didn't tell him if that's what you mean," said Kate. At Ben's frowning face she continued, "I'll tell him this weekend. We'll have more time to discuss it."

"Wanna grab some lunch?" asked Ben.

"Oh, I'd love to but I've got a doctor's appointment. How about Monday?" she asked. Never in a million years did she think she would actually ask Ben for a raincheck, and yet it had slipped out just as normally as anything.

"Deal," said Ben. A big smile came to his face. To avoid an awkward moment, he turned to exit her office.

Just as Ben walked away, in came Hank. He came in and sat on the edge of her desk. "How was your trip?"

"Good. I think we won over the client. Should be a good account," said Kate.

"Oh yeah," said Hank. "Yeah, he's already called. Good job, by the way. But, I meant how was your trip back home?" Hank lowered his head and looked up at her with raised eyebrows, as if he were waiting for a juicy piece of gossip from the coffee clutch.

"It was okay," said Kate staring at the papers in front of her that had piled up in her absence.

"Aha," said Hank, pulling away from her. "You managed to keep from killing each other I see."

"Why does everyone think we should have killed each other on this trip?" demanded Kate.

"Because everyone knows that oil and water don't mix. And wasn't it you who was huffing around here last Friday because you had to spend two days with him? You ended up spending almost a week together. That's why we're all astounded."

"Well, we did just fine," Kate said. "We managed to work through our differences and make the most of a difficult time." She wanted so badly to be finished with this conversation. She didn't want to give any juicy details. She didn't want to ever discuss that trip with anyone.

Hank looked thoughtfully at Kate and said, "It was a crazy week…unbelievable almost. I never thought I'd see something that horrific happen in our country." His eyes welled up with tears. "I was worried about you that morning, honey. I'm glad you made it back okay." He smiled and then he looked away to wipe the tears.

Kate was a little shocked by his honesty, but very moved by his concern. She sensed he wanted to say more, but was afraid to open up any further. She wondered how she was ever going to tell him about her illness. She wished at the moment she could just send out a memo to everyone in her address book and then disappear. *This is going to be more difficult than dying.*

"Hey, Hank, I'd love to stay and chat but I've got a doctor's appointment that I'm going to be late for if I don't hurry." She rose from her desk and made a move for the door.

"Yeah, sure, go ahead honey. You're not sick are you?"

"I'm fine, Hank," Kate lied and she walked out the door.

After the examination, Kate dressed and waited in the doctor's private office for a consultation. She loved his office. It always smelled so clean. The paint colors had been carefully chosen in a series of neutrals. The walls partnered with rich cherry wood furnishings and tasteful abstract art made for a very warm, comfortable space. She looked over the items on his desk. There was a picture of his wife and kids on the beach. His wife looked very young and pretty—like you would expect a doctor's wife to look. The two children were fair-headed and tanned. The picture looked like it could be an ad for sunscreen, in fact. Another picture next to that was of an older woman and she guessed it was his mother. She had a sweet face and soft blue eyes. The picture made her think about her own mother. *Oh momma, I need you now.*

Her eyes wandered over to a large paperweight made out of stone. Something was inscribed on the top, but she had to stand up and hover over it to read it. It read, "Matthew 26:39". Kate was not a Bible reader so she had no idea what the verse referenced. She would try to look it up later, if she could find a Bible. She'd never been raised with any religious beliefs. Her parents had been raised Catholic but both had rejected the Church as adults. They had refused to bring Kate up in the Church for fear it would instill what is commonly referred to as "Catholic guilt" in her. Instead they had raised her without any spirituality at all. She had no relationship with God or any higher power. She wished now that she had had just a smidge of religious education or knowledge of God to help her deal with what was happening to her now.

Just then the door opened and the doctor walked into the room. He sat down behind a large cherry wood veneer desk. "So, you had quite an adventure this week, huh?" he asked, smiling.

"Yes. Well…it was nothing compared to what those people up there endured. What a nightmare."

"Yes, you're right," he said lowering his eyes. He slipped his glasses off and looked back up at her. "Kate, we had this talk last week. I'm afraid the tests today confirm what I told you then. It's growing pretty rapidly now."

"How long do you think I have?" she asked.

"Mmm…it's hard to say. You're a very strong, healthy woman except for this damn thing. I'd guess weeks, dear." He looked sadly at Kate.

Kate held back the tears and nodded firmly in recognition of his comments. "Okay." It was all she could manage to get out of her mouth. She stood up to leave. The doctor came around and put his hand on her shoulder.

"I've ordered new pain meds for you. Enjoy the time you have left. Do some things that you've always wanted. Maybe you and Tom can take a small vacation."

Kate sighed. "Tom doesn't know yet."

"Kate," the doctor said, "It's time. He's got to know. If you love him, you have to give him the chance to prepare for this too. I know it's difficult, but remember every minute that goes by without you telling him is hurting him more." The doctor put his arms around her and hugged her gently. "Go home and have a nice evening alone with the man you love, huh? Take a pain pill, drink some wine. You could do anything after that."

The tears that Kate had been successfully holding back had breached the levee and were spilling down her cheeks as she laughed at the doctor's attempt at lightening the situation. She nodded her head in agreement. "I will. I will…tonight," she said. She turned to leave and then quickly turned back to face him at the door. "Doctor, I noticed the paperweight on your desk had a Bible verse on it. I'm embarrassed to say I don't know my Bible verses at all. Can you tell me what it says?"

The doctor looked over at the beautifully inscribed paperweight on his desk. He walked over to his massive bookshelf and took a book into his hands. He thumbed through it, until he found what he was looking for and stuck a bookmark in the page. He closed the book and brought it over to Kate. "For you," he said, as he handed a copy of the New Testament to her.

Kate was so moved by the gesture. Tears came quickly again. She hated drama, so to avoid what could turn out to be a very heavy scene, she took the book in her hands, said her thanks in a very genuine manner and left his office. As she reached the sidewalk outside of the building, she looked for a nearby park bench. She sat down and quickly opened the book to the marked page and read.

Going a little farther, he fell with his face to the ground and prayed, "My Father, if it is possible, may this cup be taken from me. Yet not as I will, but as you will."

Moved by the words she read, Kate began to sob uncontrollably. She didn't care that she was in a public place, or that she might be creating a spectacle. She just wanted to cry. There was very little she knew about the story of Christ, but she knew enough to recognize this passage as his anguish for what was about to happen to him. Kate could easily relate to this feeling of helplessness and despair, and begging whatever force may be out there that could possibly take this from her. She let herself drown in her tears for a few more minutes before finally wiping it all away with a tissue and begin her trek back to her office.

Back in the building, she began walking to her office. As she passed through customer service she found Ben entertaining two female associates by balancing a ball point pen on the tip of his nose. She rolled her eyes at the group of them. Upon seeing her, Ben dropped the pen and strolled over to her office. He came in and sat down just as she was getting comfortable in her chair.

"How'd it go?" he asked.

"Fine," she said. "No news to report. I'm still dying. Did you get the profile on Makes Scents completed yet?"

Ben rolled his eyes and flubbed his lips like he couldn't care less. "Whatever...I'll get to it. Hey, you know what I was thinking of today? I was thinking about the Painted Desert. Was that cool or was that cool, huh? Man, it was great there."

"Yes, it was, Ben, but right now I've really got to get some work done. I'm way behind."

"Yeah, okay." Taking her cue, he exited. "Lunch! Monday!" he said pointing a finger at her on the way out the door.

Kate lifted her hand and waved bye-bye to him and went back to her computer screen. It wasn't that she really wanted to work. It was the last thing on her mind actually. What she needed was time to get her thoughts together on how to tell Tom her news tonight.

Chapter 10

When she arrived home she could smell something cooking in the kitchen. Tom was a great cook—just another thing that made him perfect. She followed the smell of onions and garlic to find the man of her life standing by the stove pouring them both a glass of chardonnay. "Mmm! Something smells wonderful!" said Kate.

"Rosemary chicken over lemon angel hair pasta," said Tom proudly. "I thought you might be still exhausted from your trip, and I wanted you to take it easy. And it's the weekend now, so you can just relax and have fun!"

"Yeah!" said Kate as she lifted her glass in the air and then took a sip. It was going to take a lot of wine before she could relax.

After a fantastic dinner she asked Tom if they could just sit on the couch and talk for a while before tackling the dishes. The two of them sat down on their recently-purchased black micro suede conversation pit. Kate awkwardly began, "Tom, there's something that's been on my mind for a while and I just couldn't find a way to tell you, but…well…I just need to get it out there…"

"Wait!" said Tom holding his hand up to her mouth gently. "I think I know what you're going to say." He suddenly got very serious.

"And I want you to know that I'm going to be okay. I've thought about it and well—let's face it—it's part of life. It happens."

Kate looked extremely puzzled. "You know? How could you know? Did Ben...?"

"No. God no. Ben didn't tell me. I just guessed from your odd behavior, but who could blame you. It's been the strangest week in our lives and you were out there on the road and I mean nobody knew what was coming tomorrow or if there would be a tomorrow."

"Tom," Kate interrupted. "What are you talking about?"

"You slept with Ben, right? I knew it was a possibility. I mean I'm kind of surprised given your obvious repugnancy for the guy, but..."

"Tom!" she shouted. "I didn't sleep with Ben! Are you kidding me?"

"You didn't?" Tom looked almost disappointed.

"No!" Kate decided to start from another angle. "Tom, I was at the doctor's office today and..."

"Oh my God! Oh my God! Kate! You're pregnant!" Tom practically stood up on the couch. "That's fantastic! I can't believe it! But should you be drinking wine in your condition?"

"Geez Tom! I'm not pregnant. I'm just dying!" Kate said with exhaustion.

Tom suddenly went very quiet. "What?"

Regretting her delivery, Kate got quiet and started yet again. "It's cancer. It's a very rare form of liver cancer and there's no treatment. Tom, I don't have much time and I-I didn't know how to tell you." She wrinkled her brow and raised her eyes in hopefulness that he could accept what she was saying.

"You're serious," said Tom.

"Yes, I'm afraid I am," said Kate.

"When did you find out?"

Yikes! The dreaded question. "I found out last Friday. I should've told you, I know, but I was going on this trip, and I didn't want to tell you and then leave for two days. I certainly didn't count on being gone all week. I'm sorry, Tom. I hope you understand. I've been trying to come to grips with it myself." She searched his eyes for some understanding.

Tom's eyes darted all around the room as his mind struggled to absorb what it had just been told. "Of course I understand," he said. Then he looked back at her. He put his hands on her shoulders. "Wait a minute. No, I don't understand. I don't accept it! Isn't there something we can do? Can't we go to Sweden or someplace where they have those miraculous cures for stuff?"

Kate shook her head. "No. I'm sorry. We can't. I don't have that kind of time to go chasing possibilities that hold no promise."

"I can't believe this is happening! There's got to be something..." Tom's voice trailed off as his thoughts took over.

"I can't believe it either, Tom. It's taking a long time for it to soak in for me, too." She looked up at him and put her hands on each side of his face. "I'd like you to be there with me, Tom, but I understand if it's too much for you to deal with. Just tell me or whenever you feel like you need to back away, just let me know. I'll understand. I hate placing this kind of burden on you. I'm going to get very sick very soon. I understand if..."

"Hey," Tom interrupted. "I'm staying. We'll get through this together." He took her hands in his and raised them to his lips to kiss.

Kate wiped the tears from her eyes. "Yes, we will," she said reassuringly. "Let's just try to enjoy the time we have left."

"Oh, baby," said Tom. He held her in his arms and kissed her. "My darling, whatever you want to do...that's what we'll do." The two of them fell asleep on the couch in each other's' arms and didn't wake up until morning.

Kate woke up in a puddle of drool on the accent pillow. Somehow Tom had slipped off the couch and was in the kitchen making a pot of coffee. All Kate could think about was staying on the couch forever. It was so good to be home and have *her* coffee and *her* food and not do anything else. She was so tired of being on the road. It felt good to be still. She heard the familiar sound of washing pots and dishes. That should have been her job, but she was so tired she would let him do it.

Tom came into the living room with a tray that held two cups of coffee, a plate of cinnamon toast and some fresh fruit. "Here we are...just the way you like it." He set the tray down on the coffee table and sat next to her on the couch. He stroked her hair and asked,

"Can you believe we slept out here all night? Man! Do you feel okay? How about some coffee? That will wake you up."

Kate peeled her face from the pillow and slowly sat up so she could drink some coffee to appease him. She attempted to take a bite of toast but she felt nauseous and had to put it back down. "You know, I think I'll go take a shower to wake up," she said.

"That's a great idea, babe. You go do that and then we'll go out. I've got a little surprise for you today."

Kate smiled at him kindly, and then she rose from the couch and walked to the bathroom. She couldn't imagine what Tom could have planned for her. The last thing she wanted to do was go out. Couldn't he see how tired she was? She was already exhausted just feeling his eagerness to help her through this. She had to be grateful though. She had to appreciate his love and caring for her. It would make all the difference. She was going to have to adjust her attitude, if she was going to accept his help. By the time she was out of the shower and blow-dried her hair she had a new outlook—ready to face the day.

Tom drove them out to the mall. As he opened her door for her and walked her through the parking lot, he explained, "After this hectic week I thought you deserved some pampering, so I made an appointment for you to get your nails done." He stopped in front of the nail spa. "They're going to do your toes and your fingers. While you're doing that I've got a few errands to run. I'll be back to pick you up in an hour and a half." He kissed her on the forehead and left her standing at the reception desk where a young Vietnamese man was waiting to take her back.

"Bye," she said as he walked away.

Tom smiled at her. "Have a good time. See you soon!"

Kate turned back around and let the young man escort her to a chair to have her pedicure. She stuck her feet into the hot sudsy water, leaned back into the chair and turned on the massager. She closed her eyes and tried to let herself relax. It was not easy for her. She had never been someone to let go. As she tried to zone out, her mind brought back images of her trip. She could see herself in the desert telling Ben about her prognosis. She thought about that first day at the airport when all hell broke loose and she lost her purse. He had been so strong and in control, getting them a car and getting on the road as quickly as possible. She'd never seen Ben like that before. She always thought of him as just a big kid with no worries or responsibilities, but obviously when called upon, he could be a grown up. She thought about that last afternoon when they were dancing in Memphis and a smile came to her face.

Suddenly she heard, "Ma'am? Ma'am, wake up. We are finished with your toes." Kate jumped at the voice. She realized she had fallen asleep while they performed her pedicure. The nail technician continued, "We like you to relax but your snoring was bothering our other customers."

Kate turned red at his words. "I'm sorry!" she said. She slumped down in shame as the tech walked her to a table to have her manicure.

Just as her nails finished drying Tom walked up. "All done?" he asked.

"Yes," said Kate and she held up her hands for him to inspect the work.

"Lovely," he said. He smiled from ear to ear and his eyes looked at her tenderly. She was so lucky to have this man in her life. "I thought we'd catch a movie and then some dinner, okay?"

"Sounds wonderful," said Kate with a smile, even though she longed for an afternoon nap.

She managed to stay awake for the feature and a very lovely dinner at her favorite restaurant. But nothing topped flopping into her soft, cozy bed that night.

The next day—at her request—they took a long walk in the park. That evening Tom took her to the nicest restaurant in town.

As they sat across from each other at the small candlelit table Tom said, "You look radiant tonight."

Kate blushed. "Thank you," she replied. "It's hard not to feel lovely in a room as romantic as this is."

"Nothing but the best for my baby," said Tom. He took a sip of his cabernet and lifted his menu. "Decide what you want yet?"

"Hmmm," she said picking her menu back up and browsing through it. "I can't make up my mind. I wonder if they have anything barbecued. I'm just craving it."

Tom looked surprised. "Seriously? I didn't realize you had such an affinity for barbecue."

"Those ribs we had in Memphis—I can't get them out of my mind. The meat just fell off the bone. The sauce was sweet and tangy—just heavenly." Kate rolled her eyes upward as she imagined the delightful meal from that day.

"Do you want to go somewhere else that serves barbecue?" he asked. Tom suddenly looked nervous, and possibly a little disappointed.

"Oh no! This is just fine," Kate said soothingly. "No, I think this salmon looks delicious. I'll have that." She looked up at Tom and smiled to let him know she was very happy with his choice of restaurants. He was trying so hard.

"So tell me more about your trip," said Tom.

Kate thought for a minute before she spoke. "I would have to say that my favorite part—aside from the ribs—was seeing the Painted Desert. I mean…I can't tell you how peaceful and…serene…that's the word. It was so *serene*," Kate said as she closed her eyes imagining that she was there once again. When she opened them she expected to see Tom staring at her, but instead he was focused on something else. An extremely attractive blonde woman wearing a very short dress walked by him, and his eyes were following her backside all the way to the door. Kate was a little surprised by his behavior and stopped talking to see if he noticed. Just then Tom turned his face back to Kate.

"Sounds incredible honey. I'm glad you enjoyed it," he said smiling.

Kate was disappointed in his lack of attention but she decided it wasn't worth pursuing, so she let it go and enjoyed her delicious dinner.

After their dinner plates were cleared Tom said, "And now for dessert!"

"Oh, not for me. I couldn't eat another bite!" said Kate holding her stomach.

"C'mon," said Tom. "This caramel cheesecake looks scrumptious. How about we split it?" he asked as he snapped his fingers and motioned to the waiter.

"Sure," said Kate, giving in to his insistence. She was anxious to get the evening over, so she could tell him the secret she had been keeping for far too long.

A few minutes later the waiter brought out a cheesecake on a chilled dessert plate and two forks. He set it down between the two of them. "Wow! Doesn't that look incredible!" exclaimed Tom.

Kate looked up at it. Resting on the dollop of whipped cream was an obscenely large diamond engagement ring. Her eyes popped at the sight of it. She didn't know what to say. She looked up at Tom. She looked back at the ring. She looked back at Tom. "Tom!" was all she could say.

"Let's do it," said Tom. "What do you say?"

Chapter 11

Monday morning she was off to work again. She had to tell Hank today about her illness. She wouldn't be able to hide it much longer and she felt like she owed it to him to be prepared as her doctor had suggested. She walked into the building past the customer support center. Ben's desk was empty. He was late as usual. She went into her office, turned on her computer and emailed Hank to set up a meeting with him.

She was just getting her paperwork in order when Ben stuck his head in the door. "We're having lunch today still, right?"

"Oh...yes!" said Kate.

"K," said Ben. He smiled and backed out of the room sensing her desire to be alone.

She could hear him out there slamming the phone down. "God, I hate this job! What the fuck is wrong with these people?"

She smiled. She was going to miss listening to Ben's frustration with customers. She had no idea why he still worked there. He complained about it almost every day since she had been there. Then again, who else would put up with his laziness, his foul mouth and tardiness? He probably knew deep down that he was lucky to have employment.

Hank answered her email request with a 1:30 meeting time. *One more to go*, she thought. She immersed herself in her sales requests for the next couple of hours. At 12:00 sharp Ben knocked on her door. "Ready?" he asked.

"Yeah," said Kate. She grabbed her jacket and walked out onto the street with him. "Where shall we go?" she asked.

"I don't know. We could grab a hotdog and eat in the park."

"A hotdog? Seriously?" she asked with a wrinkled brow.

"What's the matter? 'Fraid it'll kill ya?" he asked and punched her lightly in the arm.

Kate turned and punched him back. Then she followed him to the vendor in the park and allowed him to buy her a hotdog with mustard and sauerkraut.

It was cooler than it had been the week before and she snuggled into her jacket a little tighter as they sat on a park bench.

"So, how was your weekend?" Ben asked. Mustard dripped from one side of his mouth as he spoke, but it didn't seem to bother him.

Kate forced herself to stop staring at his mustard mouth and said, "You mean, did I tell him? Yes, I told him."

"And?" Ben asked as he finished the first of the two dogs.

"It went fine," said Kate taking a delicate bite of her hotdog. "Hey, this is pretty good."

Ben rolled his eyes as if to say *I told you so*. "Fine? Can you elaborate a little more? Was he really upset? How did he take it?"

"He asked me to marry him," said Kate nonchalantly before taking a huge bite that filled her tiny mouth.

Ben stopped chewing. "Really?" he said with food still in his mouth. He waited for her to continue but when she didn't he swallowed and asked, "So what did you say?"

"I told him I needed to think about it."

He raised the hotdog to his mouth but halted taking another bite after hearing her words. "You told him you needed to think about it?" he asked. Ben put the dog down on the waxed paper and turned to face her. "You've been going with this guy for seven years and you don't know if you want to marry him now?"

64

"Well see, that's just it. We've been going together for seven years and we've never talked about getting married. Then I tell him I'm dying and suddenly he proposes. It just felt a little off to me."

"You mean like it was a pity proposal?" asked Ben.

"Yeah, I guess you could say that."

"So if he would have asked you to marry him any other time—like even last week—you would have said yes?"

Kate hesitated a little. "Yes, I guess I would have. I don't know. I mean I know I'm dying and the word forever suddenly has a whole new meaning, but I still don't want to get married for the wrong reasons. Does that make any sense?"

She thought back to the night before when she was staring at the most gorgeous engagement ring she had ever seen atop a magnificent piece of caramel cheesecake. Tom was smiling confidently waiting for her positive response. But she had not given him the response he had expected. In fact, it wasn't the response she had been expecting either. She had imagined this moment for six years down to the last detail and every time she said yes to him. But suddenly everything was different. She was full of questions. *Was Tom only doing this because she was dying? It seemed very obvious that he was. But what really frightened her was this— was he really the man she wanted to spend the rest of her life with? Why would she question that now?* Up until recently her life had a plan. Her boundaries and expectations were clear and precise. But since last Friday she was experiencing a softening of the well-defined edges she had worked so hard to create.

She tried carefully to explain her feeling of ambivalence to Tom and begged him to allow her some time to think. He graciously bowed to her request, but she could see by his disappointment that things would never be the same between them again. He went home to his apartment that night to give her some "space."

Ben let out a huge belch and wiped his face with his tiny paper napkin. "Makes sense to me," he answered. "Ha!" he laughed. "Get it? Makes sense...makes scents?" He waited for her to laugh at his brilliant play on words, but to no avail.

"I'm cold," said Kate. "Let's go back to the office."

"I've got a better idea. Let's get some hot chocolate," said Ben.

"That's a great idea!" said Kate agreeably. They walked to a corner bakery and ordered two hot chocolates to go.

Outside again they huddled together on a bench watching the kids play on the swings and slides. Kate wrapped her hands around her cup to help keep warm and let the steam rise up to warm her cold nose.

Ben turned back to her. "What are you going to do about Tom? Is he going to wait until you tell him to come back or what?" Ben asked.

Kate sighed heavily. "I told him I'd call him in a couple days, after I'd had time to think about his proposal. I mean, I love Tom. He's perfect! It's just that I need to focus on me right now and prepare for what's coming."

"So what are you going to do now?" asked Ben. "I mean…with your time?"

"I don't know," she said. "I really haven't thought that far. I guess I'll just go to work until I can't anymore and then check into the hospital."

"Are you fucking kidding me?" said Ben, mildly outraged. He turned to look straight at her. "You've just been told you've got weeks to live and you're going to go back to that shithole job while you're still healthy? How much vacation time do you have?"

Kate tried to think. "Um…two weeks."

"And how much sick time do you have?"

Kate searched her memory. "128 hours, I think," she said as she scrunched up her face to remember the last number she'd seen on her paycheck.

"Listen to me," Ben said as he took her by the shoulders. "Now this is what you're going to do. You're going back to the office today and put in for vacation and sick time. You've earned it."

Kate shook her head. "I don't want to do that. My job is the only thing I have. I'm not going to live out my days walking around the house in my bathrobe waiting to die."

"So you're just going to sit in a fuckin' ten-by-ten room in front of a computer until you die? Instead of preparing yourself for dying, why don't you try *living* while you still have the chance, Kate? When's the last time you went to the zoo, or the beach… or bowling?"

"Bowling?" she asked. "Who goes bowling?"

"Oh yeah, I forgot. You're a snob. Lots of people go bowling. Normal people go bowling."

"I'm not a snob!" said Kate defiantly. "I've just never been very coordinated. I'm completely incapable of participating in sports."

"Bullshit," said Ben. "Bowling isn't a sport. It's a game. *Anyone* can bowl. I'll teach you," he said and gulped down the last of his hot chocolate. He crumpled the cup in his hand as if it were a beer can and tossed it into the trash can. "Ready to go?" he asked.

Kate had become entranced by a vision of seeing herself trying to roll a bowling ball down an alley and his question caught her off guard. "Uh…yeah…okay," she said. She got up and threw her empty cup in the trash can.

"C'mon. This is going to be your last day at work, and tomorrow will be the first day of your *life*," he said with a big smile on his face.

Kate smiled at him. She knew he was right, but she was scared to death to admit the reality that she was facing. She wanted to continue on in her normal routine and pretend that nothing would ever change. She could see that Ben was not going to allow her to do that either. Ben took her arm to hurry her along to the office. Reluctantly she let him push her forward. She closed her eyes and took it one step at a time.

Back at work Hank was already walking down the hallway toward her office as she walked in. She heard Ben say, "Never fear ladies! Benny is back!" as he strolled back to his desk. She shook her head. She used to wonder how Tom could be friends with him. Now she was questioning how she could be friends with him. He was so juvenile. But for some reason, she felt like he was one of the few people she could trust.

Hank had always been good to her and that day was no exception as she explained her story to him. Tears fell down his scruffy cheeks while he listened. When she was finished he held her tightly and told her how much he loved her. "You were the daughter I never had," he said to her. Without any hesitation he told her to quit working and go enjoy her time. She need not worry about income or insurance.

It was difficult leaving work that afternoon, knowing she would never return. It had become her second home in the seven years that she'd been there. She felt like a fish out of water as she got into her car and drove back to her house. She let out a heavy sigh and wondered *what am I going to do now?*

A dozen red roses were sitting on the kitchen counter when she walked into the house. The note said:

Missing you already...Tom

Missing you already? What did that mean? She knew what he meant, but still it sounded a little weird knowing she was going to be non-existent soon. She poured herself a glass of wine and stuck a frozen dinner in the microwave. She stared at the flowers and re-read the note while her dinner was cooking. *Why was she so afraid to say yes to him?*

As much as she missed having Tom's wonderful cooking when she arrived home, she was kind of enjoying the quietness of being alone. She ate her dinner on the couch in front of the television and then took a long hot bath with lots of bubbles. Once her fingers and toes were good and pruned, she stepped out of the tub, slipped into her nightgown and crawled into bed. While she lay there watching TV the phone rang. Certain it was Tom, she answered with, "They're lovely."

"Thanks. Were you referring to my eyes or my legs?" a familiar voice asked. It was Ben.

Completely startled and embarrassed, she replied, "Ben! Oh, I thought you were Tom. He left me a dozen red roses on my kitchen counter today. I thought for sure it was him calling."

"Sorry to disappoint you. I tried to call your cell phone but I got some weird message."

"That's because I had it turned off when it was stolen. Remember?" she said. Oddly enough, she wasn't *that* disappointed to hear his voice on the line.

"And you didn't get a new one?" he asked.

"No. I didn't see any point," she said.

"Tom called me tonight," he said. "He's pretty torn up. I told him that he should just give you a little time and things would be fine. He has to realize that you're the one who has to go through it all. We're just bystanders."

"Wow, Ben, that was really insightful," Kate said gratefully.

"Hey, I am not completely without heart," he said. "Red roses, huh? That's weird. So what are you doing right now?"

"Just scanning for 'I Love Lucy' reruns," she said laughingly. Then she stopped laughing to ask, "What's weird?"

"Turn on channel forty-two. They've got her on a loop," he offered. "She's about to pull that huge loaf of bread out of the oven!" He laughed. She could hear him crunching on something as he was talking—potato chips she imagined.

Puzzled, Kate asked again, "What's weird, Ben?"

"Huh?" he asked. "Oh, I was just surprised he gave you *red* roses. Everyone knows you like *lavender* roses."

Ben was right. Lavender was her favorite. It had been ever since she'd seen them one day when she and Tom were walking through the flower district. She thought they were the most beautiful thing she had ever seen—the delicate, romantic, softness of the lightest shade of purple mixed with the strength and beauty of a rose—it was the perfect combination. Tom bought her a dozen of them on the spot that day. It hadn't occurred to her that Tom had neglected to bring her favorite this time. She tried to think back to the last time he *had* remembered.

"So what are you going to do tomorrow?" he asked, breaking the silence on the phone.

"I don't know. This was your idea. What should I do?" she asked.

In between handfuls of chips, Ben said, "Do something you've never done before…which should be easy for you, because I don't think you've really ever done much of anything except go to work and date Tom."

"Ha ha. Very funny," she said, knowing that it was exactly the truth.

"Okay," he said chuckling at himself. "You really want my help?"

"Yes," said Kate. "Here's your chance. Show me how to *live*."

"Okay." He paused for a moment, thinking. "Tomorrow morning get up, get yourself ready, and then wait for my instruction. I'll be in touch. I gotta go now. Need to think about this," he said as he smashed another handful of chips into his mouth. "Goodnight."

Perplexed by his vague proposal, Kate sighed heavily and reluctantly said, "Goodnight," and placed the phone back on the cradle. She laid her head down on her pillow and rolled over on her side so she could see the TV. She watched as Lucy shoved countless chocolate candies into her mouth and her blouse to keep up with the

69

speedy conveyor belt. She laughed. *It's still funny after all this time*, she thought to herself. Then she closed her eyes and fell asleep.

Chapter 12

In the morning she dressed in jeans and a t-shirt for a change. She had no idea what Ben had planned for her, but she wanted to be comfortable for whatever it was. She was pacing the floor waiting for his call when the phone rang. He said, "Go to your car." He hung up.

She went out to her car and found a package on the hood. She opened it to find two cassette tapes—one marked "1", the other marked "2". There was a cell phone, and a note that read:

Go to Eddie's Diner on 12th Street. Sit at the counter and order the French toast. It is to die for!

"Poor choice of words," she thought to herself. But then again, it may have been intentional, knowing Ben. She laughed out loud at the thought.

Kate sat down in the driver's seat and started the engine. She popped in the cassette tape marked "1" and waited for the music to start. Vivaldi's "Four Seasons" began playing. "So far, so good," she said as she pulled out of the driveway and headed to Eddie's.

When she arrived at the diner—a building that been there since the early 1950's—she walked inside and sat at the counter. A large man in his late 60's came out from the kitchen and asked to take her order.

"I'll have the French toast with cherries, please, and a cup of coffee." Kate said as she read off the plastic covered one-page menu.

"Comin' right up," said the man. He turned to grab the coffee pot, filled her cup, then walked back through the kitchen door.

Kate looked around the diner. It was typical. Booths, upholstered in red vinyl, lined along the row of windows looking out onto 12th Street. The counter looked original, with its gray speckled laminate and stainless steel edging. The smell of grease hung heavy in the air. This was classic diner for sure—classic and charming—like a little slice of Americana.

The large man came back through the doors with a plate of cherry French toast and set it down in front of her on the counter. "Here ya go," he said. "Enjoy."

Kate grabbed a fork and cut off a bite of the crispy fried bread covered in juicy cherries. She placed the bite on her tongue and closed her eyes as she slid the fork back from her lips. *Mmmm. All that sweetness along with the tart cherries...delicious.* She opened her eyes to see the man staring at her. Coming out of her state, she said, "Wow! This is fabulous!" She quickly cut off another bite.

The large man smiled slightly as if to say, "You're not telling me anything I don't already know."

"Are you Eddie?" Kate asked bravely.

"No. Eddie was my dad," he replied. "I'm Dave. I guess you must be Kate."

Startled, Kate said, "Yes, I am. How did you know?"

Dave replied, "Benny told me you would be in this morning and order the French toast."

"Benny?" she asked. She'd never heard him referred to as Benny.

"Yeah, I've known Benny for over twenty years. He and my boy, Gene, went to high school together."

"Oh!" was all she could say. Kate never thought of Ben being a kid in school, having friends. She didn't know why. She just never thought of Ben as anything more than who she had known from work.

"So, how long have you and Benny been friends?" Dave asked.

"Oh, we're not really friends. We work together...well..." she gave the question more thought. "I guess we are friends...too...I mean." She looked up to see a dazed look on the man's face. She was sure he was questioning her mental faculties, since she couldn't even answer a simple question. She regrouped and said, "I've known Ben for eight years."

As they engaged in conversation, she learned that Ben and Gene had been best friends all through high school. Ben went away to college after graduation. Gene stayed back and took a job in a mechanic's garage. Gene loved cars and he loved to drive fast. Two years after high school, he was killed in a car wreck. The death rocked Ben so heavily, that he dropped out of college and moved back home. Kate listened intently as Dave described the depression that Ben experienced for the next couple of years. Together, they worked through their grief and became quite close. "I couldn't love him more if he had been my own son," Dave said. He wiped a tear from his eye with a paper napkin.

Kate realized that she had completely lost track of time, as she listened to his story. Unable to put another piece of that delicious breakfast into her mouth, she asked for the bill.

"Oh! I almost forgot," he said as he reached under the counter. He brought out an envelope with Kate's name written on it. "He said to give you this."

She thanked him for the conversation, the wonderful food, and walked to the door.

"Come back and see me again," said Dave, as she opened the door to leave. "Bring Ben with you!"

She smiled politely and waved at him. She knew the probability of ever being back was slim, and she grew sad to think it would be her first and last encounter with this place and this man. She walked to her car eager to open the envelope and find what message Ben had left for her now.

She slid back behind the steering wheel and quickly opened the envelope. Inside was a note that read:

Follow my map to Marjorie's on North Avenue. Buy a large-brimmed hat for the sun and sunglasses, if you don't already have a pair.

She obediently followed his instructions and drove to Marjorie's—a store for ladies' accessories. Again, this was a place she had never visited. Kate had never been one to enjoy shopping.

The outside of the store was nothing extraordinary—a section of a blonde brick mini-mall that had probably been constructed in the 1960's. As Kate opened the door, the clean smell of fabric dyes and perfume samples met her nose and immediately invited her to come in and experience the beautiful things in life.

A woman—who was probably Kate's age, she guessed—welcomed her as she walked through the door. She introduced herself as Doris and asked how she could be of help. Kate explained that she was looking for a sun hat and some sunglasses. "You must be Kate!" the woman exclaimed.

Kate was not as surprised this time to find that this stranger knew her name already. "Yes. I am Kate."

"Ben was just here about thirty minutes ago and said you were coming to visit us. Please, have a seat and I will bring the selection of hats to you."

Kate took a seat on a soft-cushioned love seat and waited while Doris collected some hats from around the room and brought them to the counter. Among the six different styles, Kate chose a very simple straw hat with a large, stiff brim and an emerald green band of fabric wrapped around the crown.

"Excellent choice!" said Doris, as she held a mirror up for Kate to see herself sporting her new chapeau. Kate smiled at her reflection. "Now, the perfect pair of sunglasses, Kate," she said as she handed her some black plastic-framed glasses with dark lenses. Kate put them on and looked back at the mirror. "Very Audrey Hepburn!" Doris said persuasively. Kate could tell Doris was in the right business.

"I love it!" said Kate. "I'll take them both." She took her credit card from her purse and handed it to Doris. Doris smiled gratefully as she took the card from Kate and headed for the cash register.

At the register, Kate asked, "So, how do you know Ben?"

Doris looked up from her work to answer, but first she rolled her eyes upward as if to give it some thought. "I met Ben about two years ago at a party. He is such a sweetie!"

"And you began dating?" Kate asked with unexpected interest.

"Oh no," she said. "We never dated. We're just friends. Do you know, he comes in here a couple of times a year and buys his mother a birthday gift or a Christmas gift? He's just so cute, asking for my help to find just the right thing for her. I just think that is adorable. Don't you think that is just adorable?"

Kate was still trying to imagine Ben having a mother, let alone buying her gifts in a ladies' accessory store, but she looked up at Doris and nodded. "Yes, he is just adorable."

Doris handed Kate her receipt and said, "Oh, and I have an envelope for you from Ben. Here you go," she said as she reached underneath the counter and pulled out a familiar white envelope with her name on it.

"Thank you," said Kate, as she took the envelope from her. She turned and walked to the door. Doris followed her the whole way.

"Thank you for stopping in! I hope you have a wonderful day!" She said as Kate walked to her car. Kate smiled and waved to her before getting inside and starting the engine. She quickly ripped open the envelope to inspect the contents. The note read:

It's turning out to be a gorgeous day, Kate. Roll down the windows, crank up the music and feel the wind in your face. Drive to Barb's Roadhouse Café on Old 63. Ask for Barb.

Kate pushed the tape back into the player and turned the volume up loud. It was Alice Cooper's "School's Out". She smiled as the song took her back to the last day of school and looking forward to a long hot summer and carefree days. She rolled down her windows in dutiful fashion and followed the map he'd drawn to get to the cafe.

The wind felt good on her face. It was a cool day but the sun was hot. It was a perfect day to be outside. She already felt more alive than she had in weeks. She pulled into the parking lot just as the song was ending. The restaurant was exactly what the name implied. It was a roadhouse on a gravel road just outside of the city limits. A few men in cowboy hats were just getting out of their pickups and heading in for an early lunch. She felt a little out of place but wondered even more how Ben blended in here. She couldn't see him hanging out with cowboys. She walked inside as a gentleman held the door for her.

Inside she found a charming retro lunch counter circa 1950. Expecting to see exposed wood beams and a bar with wild game mounted on every wall, she was quite pleasantly surprised. Neon signs lit up the walls. The booths and barstools were upholstered in red and white, which looked sharp against the black and white checkerboard floor tile. She walked up to the counter and asked a waitress if she could speak to Barb. Without missing a beat, the waitress turned her head and yelled toward the kitchen, "Barb! Someone here to see you!"

A small-framed attractive woman with strawberry blonde hair pulled back neatly in a bun came out from the kitchen. She walked up to Kate and said, "Hi. I'm Barb. Are you Kate?"

Kate realized she had been standing there with her mouth open, so she closed it and nodded, "Yes".

Barb came out from behind the lunch counter holding a wooden picnic basket. She handed it to Kate. "Here's what you're looking for. Have a great day!" she said, smiling.

Kate reached out and took the picnic basket with both hands. "Thank you," she said to Barb. "You have a good day also." At the door, Kate turned back around, "Do I owe you something for this?"

Barb quickly answered, "No, honey. Ben took care of it." She motioned to Kate with her hand that she was free to leave. Kate smiled at her and walked back out to the car.

Inside the car she opened the basket to find a plate of fried chicken, little containers of mashed potatoes, gravy, biscuits, green beans, and what appeared to be peach cobbler. Wedged between several bottles of iced tea was an envelope. Kate quickly opened the sealed envelope and read the letter inside:

You now have Barb's famous fried chicken for your lunch today. I want you to follow the enclosed map to a secluded lake. Sit out on the dock and eat your picnic lunch. Take this time to think about what you want to do with the rest of your life. I'll call you at 3:00. Relax and enjoy!

Kate was overwhelmed by this adventure, but excited to continue. She slowly put the lid back on the basket and put it in the seat next to her. How she could even be hungry after this morning's breakfast was beyond her, but the smells coming from the basket made her want to devour the chicken before leaving the parking lot. It was going to have to wait, though. She had places to go. She pulled out the map to get her bearings, turned on the ignition, put on her sunglasses and shifted into reverse. She turned up the tape player to hear Quiet Riot's "Cum On Feel the Noize". Bobbing her head to the music, she squealed out of the parking lot and back onto the main road.

Ben had loaded the cassette with some great classic rock music, which Kate had not listened to for many years. She couldn't help but enjoy the memories it was stirring up inside of her. She thought about being a teenager in high school. Her parents were still living and life was so easy. She was taking it easy and hanging loose as the music continued. Then Blue Oyster Cult's "Don't Fear the Reaper" came on. If she knew Ben like she thought she knew Ben this was his idea of humor. *You jerk*, she thought to herself, but she smiled and drove straight ahead according to his directions.

The lake was amazing. It was completely secluded. She found the dock that he referred to and she pulled a blanket out of the trunk to make herself a picnic spot. With zero hesitation about calories or fat she bit into the first piece of chicken. She'd left the music playing in the car and the last song came on. She lay back on the blanket savoring the taste of real mashed potatoes and gravy still on her tongue when Collective Soul's "Shine" started playing. She looked up at the clouds floating above her and listened to the words.

Tell me, will love be there?

She stretched out and closed her eyes. *Oh God, please give me a sign...* she thought to herself.

As the song disappeared into silence, she began to focus on the sounds of the birds on the lake. She could hear a fish jump and make a splash, and just the tiniest of waves lapped at the posts of the dock. It was so peaceful—almost as peaceful as the Painted Desert had been. *What do I want to do with the rest of my life? Hmmm...I don't want to do anything but this.* She drifted off to sleep with her new sun hat over her face.

The sound of her new cell phone ringing woke her up. She scrambled to find it in the folds of her blanket and pushed the button to answer. "Hi," she said trying to sound like she hadn't been sleeping.

"How's it going?" Ben asked. "Having a good day?"

"I'm having a great day. This is just what I needed."

"I've got one more stop for you to make. Are you ready?"

"Sure," she answered.

"Piedmont Park," he said. "Can you find it? Go to the soccer fields."

"Yeah, I know where that is. Okay. I'll leave now."

"Have fun," he said and hung up.

She gathered her things together and headed to Piedmont Park. She couldn't imagine what else he had waiting for her. She drove off in anticipation of her next stop on the adventure.

When she arrived at the park she walked over to the soccer fields. There were hundreds of kids out there for soccer practice. Now she wondered what she was supposed to look for or who she was supposed to find. He hadn't told her. She was just about to get her phone out and call him back when she spotted him on the field. He was coaching ten-year-olds' soccer practice. He waved to her as he saw her walk up and motioned for her to find a seat on the bleachers with the parents. She sat down and watched while he herded young boys around and taught them how to properly kick a soccer ball. She had no idea he did this. It was incredible to see him in such a grown up role!

"I'm impressed," she said to him as he walked up to her after the practice. "I didn't know you coached soccer."

"Yeah, well, my neighbor's kid was on this team and they lost their coach last year. He sorta talked me into helping them out, and I just decided to stay. It's fun. The kids are great and it gives me something to do." He said modestly. "So you had a good day, huh? You didn't 'fear the reaper'?"

"It was a perfect day. Thanks Ben. I don't know how you pulled all that off, but I really appreciate it."

"You're welcome. I see you actually got some sun," he said, as he touched her quickly on the tip of her nose. "Wanna get something to eat?"

"Are you kidding? After that huge lunch?" she asked holding her stomach. But out of curiosity, she had to ask, "Where were you thinking about going?"

"I know this really great taco place," he said. "Come on, I'll drive." They walked to his car.

As she reached for the door handle she got a quick look at the interior of his car. There were candy bar wrappers, empty bags of chips, and empty drink cups lying everywhere. The dashboard was heavily covered with receipts, junk mail and what appeared to be parking tickets.

"Why don't we take my car?" she asked over the top of the car.

Ben sat down in the driver's seat, reached over and grabbed a handful of trash that was lying on the passenger seat. He tossed it into the back and looked at her through the passenger window as she stared with trepidation. "What?" he said. "It's fine. Get in." She carefully slipped into the car and closed the door. She stared straight ahead and didn't say another word until they arrived at the restaurant.

She bit into a luscious combination of beef, cheese, peppers, tomatoes and onions surrounded by a crispy tortilla shell. "Mmm…" she said. "These are the best tacos I've ever had." Her illness had left her with a very small appetite, but she could not refuse tasting all these wonderful flavors she had not experienced before. Just a few bites left her satisfied.

She looked over at Ben as he devoured his second taco. Something was different about him but she couldn't figure out what it was. "So how did you pull this thing off today? How were you able to get all these people to help you make this day happen for me?" she asked.

"I know people," he said confidently.

"But you must have been up all night calling people, planting notes and putting together that music mix for me."

"Not really. Well…I was up last night putting the tape together, but other than that I did everything just a few steps ahead of you. I called in sick today." He took a huge bite of taco and sauce went all over his cheek.

"You called in sick for me?" she asked. "You didn't have to do that."

"It was my pleasure. You know I don't give a shit about that place." He picked up his napkin and wiped the sauce from his face and said, "I took off tomorrow too. I got to thinking, why should I waste these great days inside at work. I might as well get out and enjoy my life too."

He's using his napkin. That's what was different. *He is actually eating like a human being and not a Neanderthal.* She noted all this while she listened to him. "Well…yes…of course. So, what are *you* going to do tomorrow?" she asked.

79

"Well, I was thinking about the zoo. I haven't been there since I was in high school. It might be fun." He looked at Kate to see her reaction. When she continued to sit there without saying anything, he finally said, "Oh…did you want to come with me?"

"Well…okay…yeah…I think I'd like to go," she said. She had been hoping he would ask her, but she didn't want to sound like she was desperate. *Who am I kidding?* She thought to herself. *I am desperate. I'm a dying desperate woman without any friends…without any life…*

"Okay then, we better get going if we're going to have any energy tomorrow," he said getting up from the table. "I'll take you back to your car."

Kate rose and walked with him out the door. When he dropped her off in the park by her car, she thanked him again for the wonderful day. "It was very thoughtful of you to do this," she said. "You obviously have some really great friends who could help you get this all coordinated so quickly."

"Eh, I just called in some favors," he said. "Have a good night. See you in the morning." He got into his car and waited for her to drive away before he left.

When she arrived home, she realized just how tired she was. She took a hot shower and crawled into bed. She felt like she could hardly keep her eyes open and wondered if it was the illness just wearing her down. A pain in her side reminded her that she'd neglected to take a pain pill at dinner. She popped one in her mouth and swallowed it with the glass of water on her bedside table. She turned on the TV. The news was broadcasting the footage of the twin towers still. They were blaming Muslim terrorists for this horrible thing and kept mentioning a name of Osama Bin Laden. She had no idea what it was all about. She had never paid that much attention to foreign affairs or any kind of news for that matter. It just didn't make any sense, and it was frightening. She'd had enough so she switched the channel. *Wuthering Heights* had just started and she snuggled into her covers to get comfortable and watch it. It had always been one of her favorite movies.

As the credits rolled and Heathcliff carried Cathy up the hillside, she wiped the tears from her eyes and turned off the TV. She lay there in the dark thinking about the story. She'd forgotten how intense a love story it really was. *I've got to call Tom tomorrow*, she thought. *It's time.*

Chapter 13

In the morning Kate awoke feeling tired still, but she refused to stay in bed. The sun was shining, and she was going to have a fun day at the zoo. She dressed in jeans and a t-shirt again, ate some breakfast, and waited for him to ring her doorbell. She had a little dizzy spell as she went to answer the door, but she ignored it, assuming her breakfast had not had time to bring up her blood sugar.

She stepped into his car and immediately noticed the absence of trash. The dashboard was completely wiped clean. The wrappers, bags and cups were gone. In fact, she almost thought he might have vacuumed the seats and carpet. He leaned over and handed her a container of anti-bacterial wipes. She started laughing. She threw them down on the floor behind her seat as he backed out of her driveway.

It was a perfect day for a visit to the zoo. They caught the elephants getting their morning bath and the apes playing with their babies. They ate an ice cream cone while they watched the lions snuggle against each other for a midday nap. "Do you think we have souls?" Kate asked as she licked her vanilla ice cream.

"I'd like to think we do," said Ben. "I hate to think that this is all there is. I mean it's so hard to believe that something of us doesn't continue on—our thoughts, our connections to others—just seems like there has to be a place where those things go. You know? How can they just cease to exist?" He took the last bit of sugar cone and ice cream into his mouth and swallowed. "I can tell you this. I'm counting on you coming back to haunt me," he said without looking at her.

She looked up at him and squinted in the sunlight. She put her hand above her eyes to see him more clearly. "You're serious?"

"Of course," he said looking down at her. "I'd rather have you creeping me out than for you to just leave me alone."

She looked into his eyes. She was finding it difficult to believe that something so sweet and serious could come from him. He couldn't hold her stare, and he looked back at the lions to lighten the heaviness of emotion he sensed.

Kate felt dizzy again. "I think I need to sit down," she said wearily.

"Are you okay?" he asked as he led her over to a park bench. "Do you need some water?"

"I think I'm just overly tired. I stayed up late last night to watch a movie and I shouldn't have," she said while she rubbed her temples. There was an overall sense of "things-not-right" today, but she didn't want to say anything that might spoil the fun she was having.

"You may be dehydrated from the sun. I'm going to get you some water, and I'll be right back."

He returned shortly and handed her the water. She gulped it down. "You're right. I bet that's all it was. I already feel better. Thanks."

"So Heathcliff kept you up last night, huh?" Ben asked.

"Yes," she said, and took a double-take at Ben. How could he possibly know? "I couldn't help it. It's one of my favorite films," she said still wondering who this person was in front of her.

"Mine too," he said.

"Oh stop it!" she said. "Now I know you're joking."

"No. Seriously, it's a great story. I stayed up and watched it last night too. It's incredibly well written. Talk about classic lines! And the acting is so intense. Can you imagine if we talked like that all the time?" Ben took Kate's hand in his and in an overly dramatic fashion quoted Bronte's Heathcliff, "'Take any form - drive me mad! Only do not leave me in this abyss, where I cannot find you!'"

Kate laughed at his feeble impersonation of Sir Laurence Olivier as Heathcliff. Ben laughed also. He pressed her hand to his lips, kissed it and then let it drop back to her lap. Kate stopped laughing. She didn't know how to respond to his action, but Ben saved them from any more awkwardness by suggesting they get lunch.

"Great idea!" she said. They left the park bench and strolled over to the café in the zoo for a bite. While they feasted on hamburgers and French fries, Kate announced, "I'm seeing Tom tonight."

Ben stopped eating. "Oh? Did you decide what you're going to tell him?"

Kate put down her burger. "I've decided to marry him." She paused for a reaction from Ben.

He nodded and said, "Good! See? You just needed a little time without him to realize how much he meant to you. I kept telling him that would happen. This is great news." He picked up his burger and continued to eat.

"It's just that I realized last night after watching that movie that love is really the only thing that matters in this life," Kate said. "It doesn't matter whether I die without skydiving or going to Europe or even learning how to bowl." She smiled. "It's whether or not I've been in love and had that love returned. And it hit me that I have the most perfect man who loves me. He's ready to marry me and just waiting for my response. That's when I decided I should do it."

"Exactly," he agreed without taking his eyes off of his burger. In between bites he asked, "What time are you meeting him?"

"I'm not exactly meeting him. I decided to just show up tonight at his apartment after work and surprise him. I thought I'd just plan to get there a little after 5."

"Well, then we better hurry up and get you home," he said as he quickly finished his bag of fries. "You've got to get cleaned up. You don't want to see him smelling like a gorilla." Ben seemed to pick up his pace after the conversation—gathering up their paper and cups for the trash. Kate felt as if she were being pushed to get out the front gate and into his car.

As he drove, Kate looked over at Ben. "Ben, thanks for today. It was such a lot of fun. "

"Yeah, it was fun. I'm glad you had a good time," he said without ever looking at her.

As he left her in the driveway, she turned back to lean in his window and said, "Thanks again for two wonderful days. You've been a great help to me. I'll never forget it."

"Hey, no problem," he said. "Tell Tom I said hi."

"Okay." She walked to her door. She turned around and waved to him as he was backing out of the driveway. She marveled at how their friendship had so quickly developed, and she was still astounded to find that Ben had more depth to him than she had ever realized.

She stepped inside and darted straight for the shower. She curled her hair and put on her little black dress. The dress reminded her of being in California with Ben. He had taken her to that little dive of a restaurant and she'd almost eaten a cockroach. Looking back now she laughed at how angry she was at the time—about what? It was just a bad restaurant experience. It really hadn't been worth getting so angry. She thought about the trip cross-country and the things she had seen, done and tasted for the first time. She had been so resistant to trying anything new. She might never have done any of it, if it hadn't been for Ben.

It was almost five o'clock and she hustled out the door and got into her car. Tom lived in a very posh apartment building downtown. A few years earlier a developer had bought up some old abandoned warehouses and turned them into lofts. She pulled into a parking spot near his building and rode the elevator up to his floor. Just as she reached his door she realized she was perspiring. She was nervous. Her head was dizzy again and now she assumed it was because of her anxiety. Her toes were numb. Was that anxiety or were her shoes too tight? She took a deep breath and knocked on Tom's door. After a moment or two she knocked again wondering if she had done the right thing by trying to surprise him. For all she knew he had decided to go out after work. Just then she heard him turn the lock. He opened the door wearing nothing but a towel.

"Kate!" he said surprised. "Wow! What are you doing here?"

Kate smiled at his astonished expression. "I decided to come by and surprise you. I thought we could talk about your proposal." When he didn't make a move she asked, "Can I come in?"

Tom said, "Well, I was just about to step into the shower…"

"Tom?" a voice from the other room said.

Kate looked at Tom with a puzzled expression, wondering if she really had just heard that. Tom looked at Kate and blushed. His eyebrows knitted together in disappointment, and then he laughed a little and said, "I wish you would have called first."

Kate stood there in disbelief with her chin dropped to the floor. Her eyes caught a movement in the room behind him as a tall, beautiful, blonde woman wrapped in a bath towel came into view. The tears rose in Kate's eyes along with the anger she was feeling. She wanted to call him every name in the book. She wanted to kick him in his crotch or punch him in the face, but she could do nothing. She whirled around and headed for the elevator.

"Kate!" she heard him call but she just kept walking. At the first floor she walked out the front door. Another dizzy spell came over her, and everything went dark as she collapsed in front of the door man.

Chapter 14

When Kate woke up in the hospital, Tom was sitting by her bed asleep in a chair. It was early morning. The sun was just peeking above the horizon. A knock on the door startled Tom awake. Her doctor came walking through the door.

"Hey! How's it going this morning?" the doctor said.

Kate was confused. She struggled to recall her last memory. It had been of Tom. She remembered being very upset, because she had seen Tom. Then she remembered the sight of that gorgeous blonde woman dressed in his monogramed towel standing behind him. She felt the blood rise as all the memories came flooding back to her.

The doctor walked over to Tom and shook his hand; then he sat down on the side of her bed and explained to her that she had collapsed. An ambulance had brought her to the hospital. They had run several tests on her during the night as well as a CT scan on her head. The doctor reached out and held her hand. "Kate," he said. "The cancer has spread, hon. There's a tumor pressing on parts of your spinal cord that will be causing dizziness and loss of consciousness. You may experience some tingling or numbness, too."

"I had several dizzy spells yesterday. I just thought I hadn't eaten properly," she said laughing nervously. She ran her fingers through her hair as she tried to absorb this new information. Tears were forming and she tried to hold them back but soon they were streaming down her cheeks uncontrollably. Between this and what had transpired last night, she wasn't sure how long she could keep from coming unglued. Her mind raced but she tried to focus on what the doctor was saying. She felt like someone had pushed her down a dark hole. She was falling and falling with nothing to grab onto and pull herself back up. She closed her eyes and laid her head back on the pillow in despair. She looked over at Tom again. Why was he here? She was so angry with him. She needed a lifeline right now, and he was the furthest thing from that.

"Well," the doctor said. "The good thing is you're here now and we're going to take good care of you." He looked over at Tom who was listening in disbelief. "We've got to do what we can to make our girl comfortable now," he said to Tom. Tom nodded in agreement but kept silent.

Kate wiped the tears from her eyes and said, "How long do I have?"

The doctor took a deep breath and let it out slowly. "It's really hard to say, but it seems to be moving very rapidly...faster than I expected." He looked at Tom and then back at Kate. "A week—maybe longer, now that you're here and can get some rest." He gave her a tight-lipped smile. "I'm going to let you two be alone so you can talk. If you have more questions, just have a nurse page me. I'll be making rounds this morning." He patted her hand and then excused himself to go check on other patients.

Tom came over to the side of her bed, sat down and held her hand. "How are you feeling? Can I get anything for you?" he asked.

"Could you get me a new life?" Kate asked as she looked up at the ceiling in exasperation.

Tom chuckled at her question. "Oh, I wish I could, baby."

A nurse walked in and took her temperature, checked her vitals, and asked if she wanted some breakfast. Kate said she wasn't hungry. The nurse told her she would bring her a menu so she could order whatever she wanted when she felt like it. As the nurse walked out the door, Kate watched as Tom's eyes followed the young woman out of the room. It was all coming back to her now. "Tom?" she said.

Still distracted, Tom said, "Huh?" He turned back to look at Kate. "What is it darling?"

"I think you should go."

Tom looked at her seriously. "Baby," he said. "I'm sorry about last night. I was lonely without you and Kristen...my...my neighbor came over and asked if she could use my shower. It was all very innocent. You just showed up at the worst possible moment."

Kate stared at him. "How stupid do you think I am Tom?" She paused for a moment and then added, "I guess I must be pretty stupid." She looked back at him. "How long have you been cheating on me?"

Tom took her hand in his. "I wasn't cheating on you, baby. It was a moment of weakness. Honestly it will never happen again."

"Tom," Kate started sweetly. "I've worked for a fragrance company for eight years now, and I recognize bullshit when I smell it." Kate pulled her hand away from him. "Why did you ask me to marry you, Tom? We've been together for seven years and you never asked. Why now?"

Tom looked defeated. "I thought that's what you wanted. I thought maybe it would give you a sense of peace at the end of your life."

"A sense of peace? To know I'm married to a lying, cheating bastard?" Kate asked with her voice beginning to rise.

"Kate, you shouldn't let yourself get so excited. You're sick and you need some rest. There's no point in fighting about this now."

She leaned back against her pillow and looked away from him. "What's my favorite flower, Tom?"

Tom looked at her to see if she was joking. He smiled confidently. "You have always loved roses."

Kate looked back at him and said, "Yes. But what *color* of rose is my absolute favorite?"

Tom looked at her with a helpless expression. After a momentary pause, he said, "Is this a trick question?"

Kate's face turned beet red as the regret of wasted years flashed before her. How could she have been with this man for over seven years and still not know him? How could he not know her? For God's sake, Ben knew her better than... She suddenly looked up and said,

"Tom, you know when Ben and I were stranded on that car trip back to Atlanta?"

Tom nodded quietly and gratefully, she supposed, because she was ripping him apart for not knowing her favorite flower.

"I told Ben about my cancer on that trip, "she said.

Tom replied, "Well, it's only natural you would tell him on that trip. After all, you were stuck together all those days. You'd witnessed a horrible ordeal with the terrorist attacks. You had no idea if your own lives were in danger. It makes perfect sense that you would feel the need to let that secret out, and release some of that toxic energy you were holding inside."

"Yes," said Kate. "You're right. And I really appreciate your understanding the situation that way. But, Tom, I kept that secret from you for almost a year, before all this happened. And while I was in the midst of this tragic situation—witnessing terrorism, not knowing what might happen to us next, wondering if I'd ever make it home to you— I had the opportunity to tell you, too. But I didn't."

Tom looked at her. She could tell he was not making the connection with what she was saying,

When she realized he had no response, she continued, "Tom, I see clearly now that you and I have never truly been intimate with each other. We've been together for years, but never really connected. And I'm not blaming you for anything. We were both at fault. I just didn't see it until now."

"What are you saying, Kate?" asked Tom innocently.

"I think you should go, Tom. I think it's time we both get on with our lives and really live while we've got the chance, "she said slowly, but confidently. She could feel the tears in her eyes as the truth fell out in front of her.

"But, Kate, honey, I can't just leave you here! Let me be here for you and help you through this!" Tom said with tears in his own eyes.

"Thank you, Tom, but no," she said graciously. "I don't need you." She smiled at him—finally realizing some peace that this was the truth.

Tom stood up and walked to the door. He wiped the tears from his eyes with the back of his hand. With his hand on the door knob he turned back to look at Kate. "I'm sorry," he said. He opened the door and walked out.

The final thump of the door shutting left Kate in a stillness that she had never experienced—even in the desert. She was now completely alone. But the thought of that—strangely enough—didn't frighten her. She sensed a new chapter beginning in her life—as if the previous thirty-nine years had been the first one. That left a week…maybe…to finish the second and final chapter.

Just then she heard a light knock on her door and it opened revealing Ben's smiling face. She immediately brightened up when she saw him. He instantly saddened looking at her tear-stained face and came rushing to her side. He took her hand as he sat down on the side of her bed.

"Tom called me this morning," he said.

"You just missed him leaving," she said. "Did he tell you everything that happened last night?"

He ran his fingers through his hair nervously. "Yeah, then I told him he was a dick, and I hung up on him. I came as fast as I could. I can't believe he had the nerve to stay with you all night, but I guess I'm glad he did. I'd hate to find out that you were here all alone."

"We had a good talk this morning," she said with a smile. She wiped her runny nose. "We broke up," she said with a little laugh.

Ben laughed, but then quickly became serious. He put his hand on hers. "I'm really sorry this happened, Kate. I'm kicking myself for not cautioning you yesterday about surprising him like that."

"Wait a minute," said Kate suspiciously. "Why would you caution me not to surprise him? Did you know?" Ben said nothing. She took a deep breath as the realization hit her. "You're his best friend. Of course you knew, didn't you?" she asked. Suddenly she felt angry again. "I can't believe you never told me. I've known you for years. How could you let me go on and on about how perfect he was and not say anything to me?" She pulled her hand away from his and crossed her arms in front of her.

"Hey," Ben said grabbing her arm. "Did you forget that up until a few days ago I was the person you hated most in this world? Why the fuck would I tell you anything?"

Kate looked him straight in the eyes. She couldn't believe he was saying that to her, but she had to agree that he was right. She couldn't think of what to say back to him.

Ben put his arms up on her shoulders. "Kate, I always knew Tom liked the girls. I knew he was a flirt and messed around, but honestly, I didn't know he was cheating on you." He looked deeply into her eyes seeking some forgiveness. He continued apologetically, "I should've known. I should've found a way to tell you. I'm so sorry."

Kate pulled back from his embrace. "Ben, I'm scared," she said suddenly.

He leaned over and put his arms back around her. He ran his hand down the back of her head in an attempt to sooth her and said, "Shhh…it'll be okay." He held her tightly against his chest.

"I don't want to die alone…in here. I can't stay in here." she said.

He pulled away from her. "Well, you're a grown woman. If you want out, then get out," he said encouragingly.

She smiled at him and nodded. "Okay," she said. She rang for a nurse and when she arrived, told her of her plans to be released. The nurse was hesitant and tried to tell her that she should be in a hospital so they could monitor her. Kate would not listen, and she demanded that they get her release papers together. After some relentless coaxing from both Kate and Ben, she finally agreed to speak with the doctor. Dr. Kent gave her a stern warning that there would be more blackouts. She was not allowed to drive anymore, and she should come back to the hospital the minute she had another episode. With that said, the doctor signed her release. Two hours later Kate was walking out the door with Ben.

"So what do you want to do now?" Ben asked, opening the car door for her.

"I want to go home, take a shower, put on some normal clothes, and go bowling," she said with a smile.

Ben laughed at her and closed her car door. He drove her back to her house and waited while she showered and dressed. Kate was happy to be home again. She let the warm water run down her face as she thought about the events of the night before and this morning. It all seemed like a dream—a frightening dream—from which she wanted desperately to awaken. As she stepped out of the shower and dabbed her face dry, she looked at her reflection in the mirror. When had her complexion become so yellow? And the circles under her eyes—she'd never noticed them so pronounced as this morning. The nightmare was becoming more and more of a reality. She suddenly realized how tired she was.

"Ben?" she yelled from the bathroom. "I changed my mind about bowling. Maybe we could just go for a walk in the park."

"Anything you want," yelled Ben back in response.

Life had certainly thrown her some curves lately. She would never had guessed that Tom would be unfaithful—maybe even more than finding out she was dying young—but she certainly never thought that Ben would end up being her friend...her best friend...her only friend.

It was hopeless trying to disguise her coloring with makeup. She would have to rely on sunglasses to mask her sallow appearance. She dried her hair and dressed quickly to meet Ben in the living room. The two of them stopped at McDonald's for lunch on their way to the park—per her request.

There was a chill in the air—the kind that whispers thoughts in your head, like "Pumpkins, Halloween, flannel, bonfires, and crispy, colorful leaves." Kate took a deep breath of the changing air. She could almost feel the cold autumn air wrestling with the soft summer air as they both passed through her nostrils and into her lungs. She snuggled tighter into her cable knit cardigan she had decided to grab on her way out the front door. If the sun hadn't been out that afternoon, they might have needed winter coats.

Apparently, Ben had seen her shiver and asked, "Are you cold? Should we find a place to go indoors?"

"No," said Kate. "I like it out here. It feels good to mix with the wind." She laughed. "That sounds weird, I know, but that's how it feels to me today." She looked straight at Ben, "I feel like I'm a part of it."

"That makes perfect sense to me, Kate," said Ben soberly. Kate searched his expression for sarcasm and found none. He really understood what she was saying—maybe even more so than she did. Was that possible?

It wasn't long before Kate needed to sit down on a park bench. They sat close to each other to keep warm. Every so often the breeze would cause her to pick up on Ben's scent. As someone who had worked in the fragrance industry, it was still difficult to put a label to it. It was a warm smell of his skin with notes of soap and just a smidgeon of musky cologne. And as it came and went with the breeze as they conversed, she found herself waiting for the next whiff of it to hit her nose. She sat there wondering when she last felt so comfortable…so relaxed…so entirely contented. Ben was speaking, but she wasn't listening to his words. Her mind was filling with feelings, observations, emotions, memories, and questions.

"Kate," she heard Ben whisper. His arm was around her shoulder and very gently squeezing. She realized that she had become so still, she had fallen asleep. She felt the warmth of Ben's breath upon her head. "You've probably had enough for today. Why don't I take you home?" he asked softly. Kate reluctantly nodded in agreement. She hated for this moment to end.

As they drove back toward her house, Ben said, "Do you want me to drive through somewhere and get you some food? Or I could rent a movie to watch. I could see if they have *Wuthering Heights* on tape."

As much as she wanted the day to keep going, Kate felt exhausted. She could barely keep her eyes open. "I'm not hungry." She yawned. "I'm really tired. I think I just need to sleep."

"Okay," said Ben turning his eyes back to the road, "Whatever you say."

The days were getting noticeably shorter. By the time they pulled into the driveway, it was sunset. Ben walked around the car, opened her door and helped her stand up. She shivered as the cold air hit her. "It's supposed to warm up again tomorrow," he said, as he put his arm around her waist to keep her vertical, while they walked to the front door. She couldn't believe how weak she felt and it was scaring her. He unlocked her front door and opened it for her. As she walked inside he said, "Do you need any help? Is there anything I can do for you?"

"No, I think I'll be okay," she said, smiling at the expression of his kindness. "Thank you, Ben, for a great day." She paused and then added, "Seems like all I've said lately is 'thank you Ben'." She smiled again. "You've been a great friend to me." When he didn't respond, she said, "Well, goodnight."

"K…goodnight," he said turning to leave. Suddenly he spun back around. "I think I should stay."

Kate looked startled. "I'm okay…really Ben, "she said, although, deep down, she hated to see him leave.

"Kate, I'm not going to be able to sleep if I go home and leave you here all alone. What if you have another black out? I can't leave you. Not like this. It would make me crazy worrying about you."

Kate was extremely surprised and pleased by his concern. She also realized he was right. She really did need someone to be around in case she fell, broke her head open on something, and bled to death in the night. "Okay," she quickly agreed. She opened the door wider for him to come in. "Okay," she said again with a smile.

She set out a pillow and blanket for Ben to sleep on the couch and then went in to take a hot bath. When she came out from the bathroom, wearing her robe and slippers, she found Ben lying on the couch watching *Casablanca* on TV.

"You really do get into the old classics, don't you?" said Kate a little surprised. "I would never have figured you for a black and white fan." She sat down to watch the movie with him.

Ben sat up and turned the volume down on the TV. "My dad left us when my brother was twelve and I was ten. My mom had diabetes and she lost her sight. She always loved the old movies. I could remember when she would stay up all night watching movies like this or *Rebecca* or *Jane Eyre*. When she went blind she would still sit in front of the TV and listen to them, but if she heard me pass by she would say, 'Benny, come here and sit with me. Tell me what you see on the screen'." Ben stopped and looked at Kate. "It became a regular thing. I would sit down with her every night and tell her what was happening in the movie. Most of the time she already knew from the dialogue, but I think she liked having me watch and interpret the scenes anyway. I think she thought she was teaching me appreciation for film. I guess she was.

"Remember the scene when Jimmy Stewart and Donna Reed were on the phone together in *It's A Wonderful Life*?"

"Are you kidding? I love that scene!" Kate exclaimed.

"Yeah…everybody does," said Ben rolling his eyes. "Well, Mom would ask me to describe it as it was happening. She'd say, 'Is he going to kiss her, Benny?' and I would say 'Yes, Mom, his face is pressed right up against hers'. Kinda weird for a ten year old boy to be doing with his mom, huh?"

"I think it's sweet. It explains a lot about you," said Kate, looking at him thoughtfully.

"Yeah, you mean it explains why I look like I do. While my brother was out playing touch football all those years and developing the body of a jock, I was sitting on the couch watching movies and eating brownies with my mom, developing the body of Sponge Bob."

Kate laughed lightly. "But those are memories you will always treasure, and I'm sure your mom does too."

Ben looked at the TV set and said, "She died last year."

"Oh, Ben, I'm sorry," Kate said sadly.

"It's okay," he said with a faraway look in his eyes. Then he turned back to Kate. "You lost your parents, too, didn't you?"

"Yes," said Kate. She blushed. She hadn't thought of her mom or dad in a long time. As a child—and an only child—she had a seemingly normal and happy childhood. As she grew into adulthood, though, the comradery of the group seemed to fail. Her parents were very close with one another and continued to act more as a couple and less as a family of three. Kate felt like an outsider in the household, and as she matured, the feeling only grew stronger. It was no heartache for her to attend a college away from home. And other than the initial shock and tragedy of losing them in a fatal accident, it had not been difficult for her to pick up the pieces and move on.

Ben noticed her pensiveness and interrupted, "I'm sorry. I didn't mean to bring up bad memories."

"Oh, no, you didn't," she assured him. "I was just thinking back. Ben, what do you miss most about your mom?"

"That's easy. I miss her smell. She had long, light brown hair, and when we hugged, I would bury my nose into her hair and smell her shampoo. I miss that so much," he said softly. "What do you miss most about your parents?" he asked gently.

Kate thought for a minute. She'd been so caught up in his unexpectedly tender response. "My parents and I didn't really have a warm, fuzzy relationship," she started. Then she paused when a memory popped into her brain. "I miss kissing my dad goodnight. I miss the feeling of my lips on his scratchy cheek at the end of a day. He smelled faintly of beer, cigarettes, and after-shave." Kate's eyes welled up at her very vivid memory, and she looked at Ben. "I'd give anything to experience that one more time," she said longingly. Then she laughed, embarrassed by her explicit display of emotion.

Apparently, Ben recognized that the conversation was getting too deep for a late night, so he stood up. "You got any beer in this house?"

Kate shrugged her shoulders. "You can check but I doubt it. Tom wasn't much of a beer drinker. I'm sure there's some wine though. Help yourself to it!" She watched him walk to the kitchen. She couldn't help but feel sad for him. Ben had no one else in his life. *He must be so lonely. At least I have...* She stopped as she caught herself. *No, you have no one.*

He yelled from the kitchen, "Do you want something?"

"No thanks," she yelled back. "I'm going to bed."

Ben came around the corner just then. "Oh...okay...well...goodnight," he said. There were those sad puppy-dog eyes looking regretfully at her.

"Goodnight, Ben," she said as she rose and walked toward her bedroom door. "And thanks again for staying."

As much as she did not want to leave him, her body was forcing her to lie down and sleep. She looked back one more time.

He smiled, raised his glass of wine, and said, "Here's lookin' at ya." He winked at her and then walked back to the couch to settle in for more *Casablanca*.

Kate lay there in the darkness under her covers, thinking about the last time she saw her parents alive. She'd been home for Spring break. That sunny Sunday morning, she shoved a basket full of clean laundry into the backseat of her light blue Gremlin and slammed the door. Mom was standing in the driveway still in her bathrobe and slippers. Dad was wearing a white undershirt, some really old blue jeans, and his leather slippers. She'd long outgrown the scratchy cheek kisses. A quick hug from Mom and a "drive safely" from Dad was as good as it got. She could still see them in her rearview mirror as she drove away, their arms around each other's waist as they waved to her.

They always had each other, she thought, with just a trace of jealousy, before drifting off to sleep.

Chapter 15

It was a difficult night for Kate. The pain kept coming back despite the pain pills. She dreamed that she was climbing mountains, but no matter how hard she tried she could never make it to the top. She was exhausted when the sun began to peek from behind her curtains. She decided to get up and make some coffee, but when she tried to move, her legs wouldn't budge. She reached down with her hands and realized that they were numb. Nervously she began pounding on her legs assuming they had fallen asleep, but she couldn't get any feeling out of them whatsoever. Finally she yelled, "Ben! Ben! I need help!"

Ben came running into her room and to her bedside. "What's wrong?" he asked, rubbing the sleep out of his eyes.

"I can't feel my legs! Ben, I'm scared."

Ben pulled back the covers to expose her legs. Still half asleep himself, he began rubbing them all over. "They just fell asleep, that's all."

"I already tried that," said Kate hopelessly. "They won't wake up."

Ben looked back at her. "We need to go back to the hospital."

Kate looked up at him with a pained expression. The last thing she wanted to do was go back, but she didn't see any choice. In resignation, she said, "Okay."

He wrapped Kate up in her sheets, picked her up, and carried her out to his car. As he drove, he said, "I know you don't want to go back there, but…"

"It's okay, Ben," she said sadly. "I don't have any other choice… I know."

Ben carried her into the emergency entrance, and left her with some attendants while he parked the car. "I'll be right back," he said anxiously in an attempt to reassure her she would not be alone. As quickly as possible he returned and found that they had already placed her in a bed. He stayed by her side holding her hand until a doctor came in to examine her.

"Kate, we're going to get you admitted and put you into a room upstairs where you'll be more comfortable. I'll have your doctor come up and talk to you there in private," said a very sweet male nurse.

Ben grabbed Kate's hand after the nurse left. "Kate, I know you don't want to be here, but we'll find out more from the doctor, and we'll get you back out as soon as we can. I promise."

Kate was feeling completely hopeless again. She'd felt so free yesterday in the park. She was relaxed and happy. She wanted to feel that way again for what little time she had left in her life.

Within an hour she was in a private room upstairs waiting for her doctor to come speak to her. When he arrived he sat down on the edge of her bed and took her hand in his. He said, "Honey, the reason you can't feel your legs today is because the tumor is growing. It's pushing on some nerves right now that make your legs feel numb."

"Is it going to stay that way?" asked Kate.

"It could…or it could not," he said. "But you're going to experience more of this as the tumor continues to grow. You have to think of it as vine—not a bump. It's growing and winding like a vine. As it winds its way through your body, it's going to push on things at random, causing black outs like you had yesterday, and numbness, like today." Without waiting for her to respond to that explanation, he asked, "How's your pain level?"

"It's pretty bad," she said. "It kept me awake most of the night."

"We can do something about that," the doctor said confidently. "Meanwhile you just get some rest. I'll check back with you later in the day." He left the room.

She looked over at Ben who had been standing in the back of the room while the doctor spoke. He came over to her bed to sit with her. He held her hand in his and stroked it gently with his other hand. "You okay?" he asked.

Kate looked past him at her reflection in the mirror on the opposite wall. The dripping faucet just below the mirror shared a sink with plastic cups, a water bottle, and various other items like cotton balls and a box of disposable latex gloves. The pale-green painted wall was spattered with stains of what appeared to be dried blood, but maybe it was only coffee—she couldn't be sure. She saw her life as— soon to be— one of those nameless stains on the wall. Her eyes welled up with tears as she saw the reflection of herself fading into the ugly green wall behind her. This was all that was left.

She drew her gaze back to his hand holding hers and looked again into his eyes. "Ben, you don't have to stay here with me. This is a depressing place, and you don't need to sit in this pathetic room, watching me shrivel up and die," she said gloomily.

"Stop talking like that. I'm not leaving you, Kate," said Ben solemnly. "But you're right. This place is depressing," he said, looking around and taking in the surroundings.

"I was so hoping I could stay home." She was sweating profusely and could feel her head getting lighter. As soon as she finished speaking, she laid her head back and closed her eyes.

Just then a nurse came in to set up her intravenous medication. Ben stepped back while she poked Kate's hand and inserted the tube. She checked the bag full of clear liquid to make sure it was flowing and then said, "There, that will help you feel better." She smiled and started to walk out, but Ben caught her at the door.

Kate watched as Ben grabbed the nurse's arm and in a hushed voice said, "Listen, she wants to get out of here. She doesn't want to die in this place. What do we need to do to get her out?"

"I'm afraid that's impossible," she heard the nurse whisper firmly. "She's too sick to go home. She needs constant medical attention at this point."

"Well," said Ben calmly. "What if we get a full time nurse to treat her at home? Can she come home then?"

"Do you know what you are proposing?" asked the nurse a little louder. "That is a lot of responsibility to take on with someone in her stage of…"

Ben opened the door and gestured for her to go outside. He followed her out the door. The last thing Kate heard him say was, "Let's talk about this…"

A little while later Ben returned to her room. "Kate?" he said. Kate opened her eyes sleepily, as he continued, "I've got to go out and take care of a few things. You get some sleep and I'll be back as soon as I can, okay?"

Kate nodded and closed her eyes again. She fell into a deep sleep and didn't wake up again until the nurse came in with a tray several hours later. "Here we go," said the nurse, attempting to sound cheery despite her dragon-like personality. "Something to eat will make you feel better." She raised Kate's bed up so she was in a sitting position before placing a tray full of Jell-O, toast and clear broth in front of her. Kate felt like the sleep had done her good. Her head wasn't as foggy as before and her pain was completely gone. She knew she was hungry, because even the crap they set in front of her looked good. She dove into it quickly.

"Don't eat too fast," said the nurse. "You don't want it coming back up." After checking the drip, she walked out of the room.

Kate thought she could eat everything on her tray, but just a couple of bites of toast and Jell-O had her feeling full. With her stomach full and her head clear, she was back to focusing on how she could get out of the hospital. Time seemed to be dragging as she waited for Ben to return. She switched on her television to occupy her time. Wouldn't you know it? *Terms of Endearment* was the featured film. Kate leaned back on her pillow, sighed, and grudgingly watched. *Oh, Ben, please come back soon.*

Just before sunset, Ben walked into her room carrying a bundle of clothing. He had a smile on his face like he'd just pulled someone's chair out from under them and watched them fall flat on their rear. "How's it going?" He asked happily. "You look great! Guess that nap really helped, huh?"

Kate didn't answer. She knew the only reason she looked perky was because he had returned. "Why are you in such a good mood? What have you been doing?" she asked suspiciously.

Ben walked over to her bed and sat down. He leaned down so he was right in her face and said, "How would you like to get out of here?"

Kate's face brightened. "Really?" she asked, delighted at the prospect. "I'm getting out?"

"I've made arrangements. But you're going to have to trust me. Can you do that?" he asked.

She continued to study him suspiciously. He had that "take charge" look in his eyes. It was how he looked on September 11th while getting them out of the airport. He was in survival mode. "Yes, I can do that," said Kate, knowing she could completely trust him.

"You're gonna have to sign some papers for your release, and then I can take you home. I brought you some clothes, so you don't have to leave wearing a nightgown. I'll have a nurse come in and get you dressed after you sign the papers."

Kate watched him as he moved about and spoke. He seemed happy but there was a little bit of anxiety in his eyes too. A nurse from the evening shift arrived. She was less frightening than the one Kate had earlier. She brought the papers to her on a clipboard, and Kate signed them all happily. When she finished, the nurse took the clipboard and walked to the door. She turned around and looked back at them. "Good luck to you both," she said smiling. Then she walked out.

A few minutes later an attendant entered to remove the needle from Kate's hand. Ben left the room while she helped her get into some sweatpants, t-shirt and tennis shoes. Kate was just getting settled into a wheelchair, when Ben popped back in the doorway.

"Are you ready to go?" he asked.

"Yes," she said feeling a little uneasy about how it was going to work at home. All she wanted to do was get out of the hospital, but now that she'd been granted her wish, she was doubtful that she could manage on her own. Ben must have promised to take care of her. That would be the reason for the anxiety on his face. *Does he know what he's doing? Is he really up for what he has to do for me?* Doubt was taking over her thoughts as she pictured Ben playing nurse to her quickly-decaying body.

Ben wheeled her out to the hospital entrance. His car was pulled up close. When they reached the car, he picked her up in his arms and placed her carefully in the passenger seat. The air was warm. Ben had been right again about the weather changing.

As soon as Ben was in the car, he started the ignition and then turned to Kate. "They didn't want to release you without knowing you would have adequate access to the meds you'll need. It's not going to be easy from here on in, but you know that, right?"

Kate nodded in the affirmative. "So what do you have planned?"

"I'm not taking you home. I'm taking you to a kind of retreat house. It's a bit of trip. By the time we get there everything should be set up for you. Don't ask me where we're going. I won't tell you. Just trust me that I think you're going to like it."

Kate studied his face trying to imagine where he would be taking her. She couldn't read his expression for anything. His big, round, sad eyes looked seriously at her, yet they were filled with compassion. She knew she could trust him. He'd brought her across the country without any harm coming to her. She figured he could find a way to take her on the last leg of her journey. She smiled at him, put on her sunglasses, and said, "Let's do this thing!" She leaned back into her seat and closed her eyes. Ben laughed at her and put the car in gear. They were off on another road trip.

Chapter 16

The pain woke her out of a deep sleep. The morphine drip had apparently worn off. She wrapped her arms around her stomach and twisted and turned in her seat trying to get comfortable. As she opened her eyes, she was startled. Everything was black! Was she blind? As she put her hands up to her face, she realized that she was still wearing sunglasses and it was pitch black outside. Grateful that she was not blind, just stupid, she folded her sunglasses and set them into the glove compartment. She looked over at Ben and he turned to look at her. "Did you have a nice nap?" he asked.

"Yes," she answered. She was afraid to tell him how much pain she was in. "Where are we?" she asked.

"Just a few minutes away now. Are you okay? Do I need to stop somewhere?" he asked.

"So…you can carry me into a gas station bathroom to pee?" she asked. "No thanks. I'll hold it," she said looking out the window. It was dark and impossible to see anything but the stripe down the middle of the pavement. They seemed to be the only car on the road.

The car slowed as they came into a town. They wound through two-lane roads for about fifteen minutes and then pulled in front of a little cottage. "Here we are," said Ben. He quickly got out of the car and ran around to get her out. He opened her door and reached down to pick her up.

"So, where are we?" she asked. "Now that we're here, is it still a secret?"

"Of course not," said Ben as he carried her to the front door. There were dim lights inside, and someone was coming to let them in. The door opened to reveal a middle-aged, large-framed, black woman with a kind face smiling at them. "You made it!" she said happily. She opened the door wider so Ben could carry Kate inside. "You must be Miss Kate!" the lady said sweetly. "My name is Angeline," she continued as she gestured for them to enter the room. Kate looked all around at the interior of the cottage as they passed through it. It looked like a vacation rental. The decorations were modest but charming. The air smelled stale, and Kate figured that this house had been closed up for quite some time. "Come this way," said the woman. "I'll show you the bedrooms."

"Is it all here?" he asked her.

"Everything arrived just as you ordered," said the woman as she led them down a narrow hallway and motioned toward a bedroom.

Kate gasped as Ben carried her into the room. It was a small room with an iron double bed in the middle of it. A small dresser and desk shared the opposite wall. On the bed was a beautiful handmade quilt with an abundance of pillows wrapped in ruffled shams. But none of that was what made Kate gasp. What made her swoon at the sight was a little table next to the beautiful iron bed. On it was a vase that held a dozen lavender roses. Ben saw her looking at them with tears in her eyes.

Angeline smiled and said, "Everything just as you asked, Mr. Ben."

"I wanted them to be the first thing you saw when you woke up in the morning," said Ben. He carried her over to them and then set her down on the bed.

"Ben, they're beautiful." She leaned over and took a rose and put it to her nose to breathe in its sweetness. She closed her eyes and laid the rose softly against her cheek. Then she placed it back with the rest. She looked at Ben. "Thank you."

"There's more," said Ben, "If you still have the energy." She nodded to him to continue, and he picked her up again and carried her to the back of the cottage to the outside. Behind the cottage was a small porch with some lounge chairs. Beyond the porch lay a sandy beach and the ocean. She gasped again as she realized where she was. "You said you wanted the end to be like the movie *Beaches*. In the movie they were in California so they could sit out and see the sunset. Unfortunately the best I could do on short notice was Tybee Island, so all I can offer you is an ocean sunrise."

Kate was overwhelmed. She struggled for words to show how amazed and grateful she was. "Oh, Ben," she said as tears poured down her cheeks. She snuggled gently into his neck in an effort to hug him while he was holding her. "It's incredible! I can't believe it!" She pulled back up to look him in the eyes and asked, "How were you able to do all this?"

"Hey, I know people. Remember?" he said laughing lightly, but never took his eyes off her.

Kate didn't know what to say after that. She stared into his eyes wondering who this incredible person was and what had happened to the guy she knew for the last eight years. Her eyes were clouded by tears but she was still able to see the satisfaction he was feeling at her obvious joy. For the first time in her life, she felt like a princess in a fairy tale. She couldn't imagine that anything greater could ever happen to her. To end the uncomfortable silence and the romance of the moment, Ben said, "Come on. You can see more in the morning. You need to go to bed. Besides you're fucking heavy." Kate giggled through her tears as he carried her back to reality and into the house.

Back inside Ben finally introduced the mysterious-but-friendly woman as Kate's nurse, Angeline. She was licensed to administer any medications Kate would need. Everything that the doctor had prescribed for her was right there. Seeing how exhausted Kate was he took her into the bedroom and let Angeline get her ready for bed.

Kate was dumbfounded by all that was happening around her. She asked Angeline how she knew Ben. Angeline told her that she didn't. She helped Kate use the bathroom and then dressed her for bed. As she did so, she explained that she was a private nurse for hire, and Ben had called her agency earlier that day asking for her services. She didn't know who owned the cottage. She was just told to report there and to make sure everything was ready for their arrival. After she had Kate tucked into bed and given her some medication for the pain, she excused herself. "Now, if you need *anything* tonight, you just call me, okay? I will be right next door. If you need to use the bathroom or have something to drink or anything at all—you hear me?"

Kate smiled at Angeline and said, "Yes, I promise I'll call. Thank you."

"Okay, then. Goodnight Miss Kate. You have sweet dreams now," Angeline said sweetly as she closed the door gently.

Ben came in a short time later bearing food. "Hey, how ya feeling?"

"Better," said Kate. The drugs were starting to kick in, and her pain was diminishing. "Ben, I still can't believe that you did all this. I mean...for me."

"You're my friend. It's what friends do. They help each other out," he said as he set a tray down in front of her and sat on the edge of her bed. "You should eat." He rose from the bed and headed for the door.

"Ben," she said with a sandwich in her hand. He turned quickly. "Will you stay and talk to me?"

"Sure," he said and walked back over to the bed.

"Tell me where we are, and how you found this place, and how you made this all happen so fast!" she said.

"Well, we're on Tybee Island, not too far from Savannah. The cottage is a rental that I was able to secure after I finally got 'Nurse Ratchet' to help me talk to your doctor and make some arrangements. This was the quickest way to get you to the beach, so I just...made it happen."

The little turkey sandwich Angeline made tasted delectable to Kate, but she was already full after a couple bites. She drank a little bit of tea and then felt terribly sleepy. The look on her face of utter exhaustion caused Ben to stand up again. "I'm really going this time. You need to rest. I'll see you in the morning." Before he left he turned and asked, "Do you want me to wake you up to see the sunrise? I hear it's pretty spectacular."

Kate smiled. "That would be nice," she said, resting back against her pillows. "Goodnight Ben."

"Goodnight, Kate," he said as he closed her bedroom door.

She pulled her covers up to her chin and closed her eyes. All the stress from the day before just melted away as she drifted into a peaceful sleep.

Chapter 17

She slept calmly and deeply all night until the sunlight woke her.
The first thing she saw was the lavender roses, just as Ben had
planned. They were the loveliest roses she'd ever seen—so delicate
and the perfect shade of lavender. Her joy turned to disappointment
when it occurred to her that the sun was already up, and she had
missed the sunrise on the beach. She had to admit, though, that the
rest had been good for her. She felt better than she had in days. She
took a deep breath in and stretched as much as she could to wake the
rest of her body. Her legs were still numb, but she tried not to focus
on them. She longed to get out and soak up some sun. She called for
Ben, but Angeline was the first to come through the door.

"You need something, Miss Kate?" Angeline asked.

"Is Ben here?" Kate asked.

Just then Ben peeked in through her doorway. "Right here,
Sleepy," he said. "Hey, I'm sorry I didn't wake you this morning, but
you were sleeping so soundly, and it was a long day yesterday…"

"Don't worry about it," Kate interrupted. "I needed the sleep
badly. There's always tomorrow!" she said, and then she reflected on

how silly those words sounded at this point. Tomorrow wasn't guaranteed.

Angeline stepped into Kate's thoughts and said, "I bet you're hungry! What can I bring you to eat?"

Kate thought a moment and said, "I'd really just like some toast and a cup of tea, but I want them outside in the sun." She smiled at Ben, who couldn't seem to take his eyes off of her.

"Okay," said Angeline. "Toast and tea on the patio, it is! But first, let's get you cleaned up and into some clothes."

Ben offered to make the toast and tea, while Angeline assisted Kate in the bathroom and changed her clothes.

Sometimes the simplest things in life are the most enjoyable. Sitting in the sun with a wide-brimmed hat and sunglasses, sipping a hot cup of tea, and listening to the ocean waves break on the beach was all Kate needed to make her whole day. She relaxed and enjoyed living in the moment of tranquility. Ben sat next to her drinking a soda out of a can.

After a loud belch, Ben asked, "What would you like to do today, Princess?"

"Nothing but this," said Kate out of complete satisfaction. "Nothing but this," she said again.

"Your wish is my command," said Ben. He leaned back in his lounger with his hands behind his head.

They lunched on the patio. They ate dinner on the patio. When it was dark, they went inside and watched black and white movies on television until Kate fell asleep.

The next morning, Kate woke before dawn. The pain was strong, despite a dose of medication at midnight. Lying there in the darkness left her wondering what it would feel like when she died. *Would it be like this? Darkness? Loneliness?* She felt her heart pounding as her fears grew. Just then she heard a tiny knock on her door.

Ben walked into her room with Angeline. "Do you feel like going out this morning?" Ben asked.

"Yes," answered Kate. "I can't wait." She smiled to hide the distress going on inside her.

"Well, first we need to get you into some warm clothes," said Angeline. "It's chilly out there. Ben, you can wait outside while we get ourselves ready." Angeline helped Kate dress quickly and then

114

gave her some more medication. Kate could tell she wasn't feeling as strong today. She looked at her reflection in a hand mirror that was on her nightstand. She barely recognized the woman she saw. Sadly, she set the mirror down on the table. She wanted to cry at her misery. She wanted to wallow in her pain and sadness and hide from everyone. But there was Ben ready to carry her outside. She saw no disappointment on his face.

Ben carried her out and placed her on the wooden lounge chair filled with blankets and pillows that she had spent a large part of the day before enjoying. It felt different today in the chilly air. It was nothing like the bright warmth of yesterday. Kate snuggled deeply into her sweater and blankets, struggling to feel that cozy sensation she longed for. Ben took the seat next to her and leaned back with his hands behind his head, and they both stared out to sea as the sun became an intensely bright light that peeked out over the calm water.

Within minutes the dark sky became painted with yellows, pinks and turquoise. Kate and Ben watched as the tiny bit of light became a full sky which eventually transformed into a soft blue field that carried a fiery ball of sunlight. Kate put on her sunglasses which Ben had thoughtfully placed on a table by her chair earlier.

"How are your legs today?" Ben asked. "Any feeling come back yet?"

Kate tried to wiggle her toes and then pressed her hands into her thighs to see if she could feel them. "Mmm…no…I don't think so," she said disappointed.

"Good!" Ben said. "Then I can do this without you screaming!" He jumped up and grabbed Kate into his arms. He carried her down the beach to the water's edge and waded into the icy cold ocean. Kate screamed all the way.

"What are you doing?" she yelled while she laughed at him taking her out into the water.

"You need to get your feet wet," he said. He dipped her feet into the waist high water. "Can you feel that?" he asked.

She was giggling hysterically. "No, I can't! And I'm glad!"

"Oh, then I guess I'll have to dip the other half of you in!" he exclaimed and he began to tilt her back as if to dunk her into the rushing waves.

"No!" she screamed and wrapped her arms tightly around his neck to keep her head as high as possible. Her cheek pressed tightly against his scratchy, unshaven face, and she felt his lips graze her shoulder as she held on snugly to him. She brought her hands up to the back of his head and twisted her fingers in the wet curly strands of his hair. He stopped tormenting her and stood still now. The salty water dripped down his cheek and she tasted it as it trickled into her mouth. She liked the way he smelled, too. For the first time in her life she considered kissing him, but she stopped herself.

"It's fucking freezing out here!" he said and began walking back to the beach. He laid her back down gently in her lounge chair. He carefully wrapped her in soft blankets and tucked them in as if she were a child, before he fell back into his chair. They both lay there panting from the little jaunt. "Wow! That was invigorating," he said rubbing his cold wet feet to get the blood flowing back into them.

"You're crazy, Ben," said Kate with a big smile on her face. "That's why I like you so much," she said softly as she looked straight at him. She picked up her sunhat and placed it on her head and leaned back on her chair.

"Wow! Well, I've come a long way since September 11th when I was the most hated person on the planet, then, haven't I?" he asked.

"We were both different people at that time," said Kate blushing with embarrassment as she recalled that awful night.

"No, we weren't. I'm still the same and you are too. You've just come to appreciate my greatness that you obviously couldn't see before, because you were too busy being a bitch."

"Ouch!" said Kate. But she knew she deserved it. The warmth of the sun felt incredible, while the cool ocean breeze raced across her exposed face. She was finding her cozy place again.

"I'm just teasing you. You were never a bitch," he said. "Uptight…high maintenance…overly demanding…anal retentive, maybe…but not a bitch," he continued.

"And see, I'm none of those things now, because I'm not the same person," she said while bringing her hands up to the brim of her hat.

"No, you're still the same. You've just called on other qualities within yourself that you didn't even know you had. You're still the same person, Kate— just better," he said looking at her.

116

She thought about what he said for a minute or two before replying. "You're right, Ben. I didn't see the good in you before. I guess because I wasn't looking for it. I had no idea what a really terrific person you are. I feel like every time I turn around I'm thanking you for something else you've done for me. It never seems to end. And this cottage on the beach, the nurse, all that you're doing for me... my insurance can't pay for all this. That means you're paying for it, and it must be costing you a fortune! And in the meantime you're missing work. How much time are you taking off?"

"Ah, I quit my job the same day you left," he said looking at the waves crashing out at sea.

She sat forward as far as she could make her body bend in order to see his face. "You quit? Why would you do that? What are you going to do for money?"

"I don't need the money. I don't need the job. I could've quit years ago—just didn't" he said. He had his hands folded behind his head looking very cool and comfortable.

"Oh, yeah, sure," she said leaning back on her arms, laughing. "What, did you win the lottery and forget to tell anyone?"

"Hmmm, something like that," he replied. He looked over at her with a serious look on his face. "My dad left us when we were kids, right? Well, one day about nine years ago, I get a letter from an attorney. Seems my father struck it rich in Oklahoma. He got involved with oil companies somehow...I don't know. I didn't really care. I didn't give a shit what he did with his life. So, anyway, he died, and he left everything to me and my brother."

"And how much was that?" she asked with piqued curiosity.

"Five million...roughly," he said very casually.

Kate's jaw dropped when she heard him. "Five million *dollars*?" she exclaimed. She was completely astounded. She began to wonder if he was pulling her leg, so she held her breath, waiting for the punch line.

"Yeah, well, only half of that. The other half went to my brother," he said. "But I didn't know what to do with it. I didn't want it. I thought about donating it, but I didn't know who to give it to, so I just let it sit there and waited till something told me what to do with it."

117

"You're serious, aren't you?" asked Kate, still finding it hard to believe that this story was true.

Ben looked her straight in the eye. "Of course it's true!" he said, slightly irritated by her lack of belief in him.

Kate swallowed hard. She was stunned by what she just heard and flattered beyond belief at what she was experiencing. She thought a bit more before saying, "But Ben, you hate your job. You have complained every day that I've worked there. Why—if you had all that money at your disposal—would you continue to go to a job that you hate that much?"

Ben looked away from her and back at the ocean. "Like I said before—I hated my dad for what he did to my mom and us. I didn't want the money. I just left it sitting there in the bank, until you came along. Then I knew it would go to good use to give you all of this. I wanted to give you a good ending to your story—like *Beaches*, you know?"

Kate felt that there was much more to the story but he obviously wasn't willing to share so she dropped her questioning. This unselfish act of human kindness was unlike anything she'd ever known or ever felt she deserved. She watched him sitting there looking no different than he had looked since the day she met him. Yet, she had no idea who he was. *Who is this person sitting beside me? I once thought he was a delinquent. Now I wonder if he might be an angel.*

They sat there in silence for nearly an hour, basking in the sun as it moved higher into the sky. Suddenly Ben spoke up, "What's your favorite movie, Kate?"

Without moving Kate said, "What is the favorite movie of any Georgia gal? *Gone With the Wind*, of course."

"Of course!" said Ben, "I should have guessed it."

"How did you know that lavender roses were my favorite? You couldn't possibly have guessed that," she said.

After several minutes of silence, Ben said, "Don't you remember that day you came into work and went on and on about lavender roses? You wouldn't stop talking about them. I'm sure everyone in the office knew by the end of the day that they were your favorite."

"Ben," said Kate, "I have never come to work and gone on and on about *anything*. I hardly ever spoke to the staff."

"Yes. That's true," he said. "Everybody there was afraid of you, you know. You never spoke to them. You would just walk in to your office and stay there all day cut off from everyone. In eight years you never made a single friend at that company. They all thought you were stuck up. I guess in a way, they were right."

"Hey!" said Kate. "I wasn't that bad. Was I?" she asked remorsefully.

"Kate, everyone who worked there was a child," said Ben. "I knew them all as well as I ever wanted to, and you weren't missing out on anything. I'm just teasing about them thinking you were stuck up. They never said anything about you. Half of them probably never even knew you worked there. They were all under thirty and interested in nothing more than drawing a paycheck and where to get drunk on the weekend. There was no one there of any substance, except of course, me...and...you."

"And Hank!" Kate chimed.

"And Hank," said Ben in agreement. Hank's a good guy.

Angeline interrupted the conversation to check on Kate's condition. Although Kate felt fine, the nurse insisted on her going inside to get out of the sun and rest. Kate obediently did as she directed. She lay there in the coolness of the dark room, feeling exhilarated. It occurred to her that she might be finally experiencing what Ben had instructed her to feel—life.

The rest of the day was lazily spent grazing on sandwiches and snacks, listening to the waves crash on the shore, and ended with another black and white classic film, *It's A Wonderful Life*. The movie finished right after midnight. Kate fought off her sleepiness to see the end. She looked over at Ben sleeping peacefully on the other couch. Every so often he let out a little snore. It would startle him for a moment, and then he would fall back to sleep. She hated to wake him to carry her to bed, so she puffed up her pillow, lay her head down, and gave in to her body's request for much-needed sleep.

Chapter 18

The next few days passed on just as easily and carefree. Kate felt her body growing increasingly weaker. Medication was administered more often, which made her time spent awake shorter and shorter.

On Saturday, Ben rented a boat at the marina for them to take out and watch the sunset. As the golden light spread out across the water and danced off the marina in the distance, Kate remarked, "Remember when we were in Marina del Ray?"

"Of course, I do," said Ben.

"Remember that terrible restaurant you took me to?" she asked smiling.

Ben laughed and said, "Yes, I do. It was pretty terrible, wasn't it?"

"I thought that was your favorite place in that town? I thought that's why you took me there?" Kate asked.

"Ha! No," said Ben. "That was my first time in Marina del Ray. I had no idea where I was taking you, but then you started complaining about your feet being tired, so I just went in the very next restaurant I saw."

"What?" said Kate, startled. "Why?"

"I just wanted to spend more time with you. I was hoping to impress you with a great night out. Well, that turned out to be an epic fail," he said sadly.

"Of course, now we can look back on it and laugh, though, can't we?" Kate offered.

"Yeah," said Ben. "I guess we can."

In no time at all, the sun had completely disappeared into a moonless field of navy blue. Ben brought the boat back to the marina, and another day came to a close.

Kate woke up the next day with more energy than usual. She ate a piece of toast and drank her tea out on the patio with Ben. Despite his continuous upbeat attitude, he had been exceptionally quiet the last few days, avoiding any deep conversations. She wondered if he had become bored with being there—being with her—day after day. She knew her sad, yellow face was nothing pretty to look at every morning. Was he just waiting for this to be over? Bravely she ventured a question. "What would you be doing right now if you weren't here with me?"

Ben, who was sprawled in his t-shirt and swim trunks on the lounge chair next to her remained still as he said, "I'd be wondering what the hell I was doing with my life."

"What do you mean, Ben?" Kate asked, honestly confused by what he had just said.

"It means there's no place I'd rather be than here with you right now, Kate," he replied. "You're not keeping me from doing anything else, so stop thinking that."

Taken aback by his response, but silently delighted, she sat back and closed her eyes—completely satisfied.

Just then Angeline yelled out from the cottage, "Lunch is here!"

Ben turned around and started to get up. "Good! I'm starving! What do you say?" He bent down to gather her up in his arms.

Kate reached her arms up and placed them around his neck. "I say I'm hungry, too," she said smiling at Ben. As he carried her back to the table waiting for them on the patio Kate kissed him on his cheek. He looked at her slightly puzzled. She smiled at him again. "Thank you...for everything," she said.

On the patio was a table filled with barbecued chicken, ribs, pulled pork, baked beans, coleslaw, and fresh rolls. Kate gulped when she saw the large array of food. Ben lowered her into a chair and said, "I know you really liked the barbecue we had in Memphis, so I had the local restaurant send some over. I'm sure it won't be as good, but it'll do. Besides we've got way better scenery than Memphis!"

"That's for sure!" said Kate eyeing all of the food. Everything looked so good. She took heaping helpings of all of it onto her plate. But after one bite of the luscious tender rib, she stopped. Something was happening to her that she could not understand nor explain. She felt dizzy and out of control.

Ben noticed right away that something was wrong. "What is it?" he asked.

Kate looked down at her plate and closed her eyes. Tears began to come forward and she said, "I think I need to go lie down." She was afraid to say what she thought was really happening. She could tell that things inside her were changing. She could feel her body pulling away from her mind.

Ben dropped his fork and went over to her quickly. He lifted her up and carried her into the house asking for Angeline's help as he headed to Kate's bedroom. Angeline met them at Kate's bedside. As Ben tucked Kate into her covers, Angeline checked her temperature and pulse. Kate still couldn't put words together to explain what she was feeling. Her head felt detached from the rest of her and her limbs were tingling. She looked at Ben. "It's happening." Then she looked at Angeline and said, "It's happening, isn't it?"

Angeline looked at her soberly and nodded slightly. "You were out in the sun a lot these last two days, Miss Kate. You've probably just worn yourself out." She handed Kate a couple of pills and some water, then continued calmly. "This will help with your anxiety. I'm going to bring in a pan of water and a washcloth to cool you down. Just rest and I'll be back in a few minutes." She walked out of the room. Ben continued to sit on the edge of her bed.

"Ben, I'm scared," she said. "I feel so weak—like I'm shrinking."

Ben reached out and took her hand. "You heard her. You had too much sun. I shouldn't have kept you out so long. You'll feel better after she sponges you down, and then we can go back out when the sun is lower. It's going to be fine."

Angeline returned with a dish of water and towels. She asked Ben to step out while she bathed Kate.

"I finally get a chance to see two hot women bathing and I have to leave. Story of my life," he said as he walked to the door shaking his head. He turned around and winked at Kate just before he closed the door.

"You think that's bad. I finally found a millionaire to share my life with, and I'm dying!" Kate said meekly, but humorously.

Ben stopped for a moment to give her one last look and said sweetly, "You win," before he walked out.

Kate lay there while Angeline undressed her and wiped her down with a washcloth soaked in tepid water. It was relaxing and calmed her worried mind. Kate asked her, "Do you see a lot of people die?"

Angeline replied hesitantly, "I've worked with several hospice patients."

"Are they afraid like I am?" asked Kate. "Is it normal for me to be so scared? I mean, up until these last few days, I didn't even think it was real. I kept thinking it was a problem that I just had to deal with, but it never sunk in that I was really going to die, you know?"

"Yes," said Angeline sympathetically. "It's perfectly normal to feel what you are feeling. Most people are scared when they realize it is happening to them, but I can also tell you that there is a peacefulness that comes over them as they pass. Try to keep that in mind when you get anxious. Peace will come to you."

"Where do you think it comes from? The peace, I mean," Kate probed.

Angeline blotted Kate's body softly with a dry towel. "I think it comes from God—from seeing His presence as you pass into the afterlife." She noticed Kate's look of questioning and so she asked her, "Do you believe in God, Miss Kate?"

"I don't know," said Kate. "My parents never took me to church, and we didn't discuss religion."

"Well," continued Angeline. "Religion is one thing," she said as she tucked in the sheets below Kate's mattress. "Believing in a spiritual presence can be quite separate. But that is for you to seek out and find in your own way. All I can tell you is that I believe He exists, and He will be there for you when you are ready to come to Him."

"I'm not sure I've been good enough for God to want me. I've been a terrible person all my life. I was always so worried about making my life perfect, that I never really paid attention to other people's needs. I could be so mean—especially to Ben. I treated him horribly...more horribly than I treated everyone else...which was pretty bad. We worked together for years and I was so awful...so judgmental and condescending," she said as she thought back on all the times she had mistreated him.

"But now you love him, and he obviously loves you. So all is forgiven, right?" Angeline asked softly. She had an amazing calm, all-knowing presence to her that could not be missed.

"Huh?" asked Kate astonished by what she just heard. *Love?* She smiled at Angeline and laughed casually. "Oh no, we're not in love. Ben and I are just friends. I dated his best friend for many years. He's just been the only..." She stopped in mid-sentence. Her own thoughts were coming back to her now. *Ben is my only friend. It seems like I'm always saying 'thank you, Ben'. Who was the first person you told about being sick, Kate? Who are you here with now, Kate?* Now she was no longer sure what was true.

Angeline interrupted Kate's thoughts with a smile, "I'm all finished. I'm going to send Ben back in here to tell you goodnight and let you rest for a while, okay?"

"Okay," said Kate. "Thank you." As Angeline walked away, she left Kate in a new state of confusion. She had never once considered that there was a love that existed between Ben and her. Now she questioned herself. *Was this how falling in love felt like?* She thought back to the road trip across the country that they had taken. She thought of that day in the desert. She remembered the late night phone calls with him while they watched "I Love Lucy" episodes till they fell asleep. It occurred to her that recently every time she looked for guidance or help, she had turned to him. And even more significantly, every time she needed him, he was there. Had she really fallen for...Ben?

Ben quietly came back in the room. He sat on the side of the bed and took her hand again in his. "Feel better?" he asked.

"Yes," said Kate.

"Good," he said. "Are you sure? You look a little...unsure about something."

Kate realized then that she had been studying him from the moment he walked into the room—watching the way he moved, looking at the way he didn't comb his hair, realizing that he had the warmest brown eyes she had ever seen. She stopped herself from further interrogation and said, "I'm fine." Seeing him now she realized that all she had been wondering about was true. She smiled warmly at him.

Her smile apparently made him uncomfortable, because he suddenly said, "You should get some rest." He stood up and headed for the door.

"Ben?" she called to him. She wasn't sure what she was going to say next but she wasn't ready to let him go. He turned around to face her. "Do me a favor?" she asked quietly.

"Anything," said Ben.

"Stay with me? I don't want to be alone."

Ben blushed and said, "Sure." He began to walk back over to her side of the bed.

Nervously, she asked, "No, not over here. Will you lie down with me?"

Surprised by her request, he cautiously said, "Yeah—okay." He walked around to the opposite side of the bed and awkwardly lay down next to her.

"No," said Kate. "Not on top of the covers. Get under the sheet."

Ben lifted the sheet slightly and looked underneath. He quickly slapped it right back down again. "But you're naked under there!" he said shocked.

"Don't worry," she said. "Your virtue is safe. I'm too sick to try anything."

He studied her with a questioning look. The space between his eyebrows pinched tightly together. The look of *this is a trap* was written on his face.

"I want to be close to you, Ben. I want you next to me," she said reassuringly. She lifted the sheet as an invitation to come closer.

Ben cautiously removed his clothing down to his underwear. He pulled the sheet up and slipped underneath it. He lay there on his side, propping his head up with his left hand. He looked into her eyes thoughtfully. She reached her hand under the covers until she found his other hand. She brought it up to her lips and kissed it, then slowly slipped it back under the sheet and to her breast. Her own hand was shaking, and she surprised herself with her forward behavior. *Time is not on your side,* she heard her inner voice say. *There's no time to think, only time to move.* Ben looked at her in confusion and disbelief.

"Ben, I want to feel you, and I want you to feel me," she said quietly.

"Are you sure?" he asked timidly. With her consent he brought his face close to hers and kissed her mouth gently. His lips were full and soft, as they touched hers very briefly at first and then lingered into one long, tender, passionate kiss. She closed her eyes as he turned his attention to her body and very carefully ran his hands over her neck before sliding across her shoulder, breast and stomach. He touched her as if he were examining a glass figurine, exploring the curves and the surfaces with such amazement and reverence. As much as she was enjoying his touches, she could not stay awake, and she fell into a dream state feeling loved and admired like she'd never known before.

Chapter 19

When she woke up it was twilight. Faint flashes of pink and orange slipped through the narrow openings of the window blinds and painted her dark bedroom walls. She felt nauseous, but she wanted to fight it. She turned to see if Ben was still there. He was still on his side with his head propped up on his arm looking at her.

"Hey," he said when her eyes met his.

"Hey," she said back to him. Just then something strange occurred to her. She could feel her feet! Her eyes became round and she said, "Ben! I can feel my feet!"

"Really?" he asked excitedly as he sat up and began poking and prodding at her legs. "Can you feel this? Can you feel this?" he kept asking.

"Yes!" she kept saying over and over, as she laughed with joy of becoming "whole" again.

Although she could tell she had feet and legs again, that was the extent of it. She could move them slightly but they were still tingling as if they were asleep. "Well, at least it's some progress," she said optimistically.

Ben suggested they get dressed for the cooler night air and eat some supper out on the patio. He went to get changed while Angeline helped Kate get ready. Kate sat on the edge of her bed for the first time in many days and wished she could start walking again. *Be grateful for little things*, she told herself.

Despite her long nap she felt tired and weak, but the last thing she wanted to do was to stay in her bed. Ben came in and carried her out to the patio where he had set up a light supper by candlelight. "You don't have to eat anything if you don't want to," he said to Kate as he set her into the lounge chair and arranged her pillows to make her comfortable. "I just brought out little bits of everything I could find from the fridge."

Kate nibbled on some shredded chicken from the barbecue that was supposed to have been her lunch, but a few bites were all she could handle. "I guess I'm not as hungry as I thought," said Kate trying to avoid the obvious state of reality.

Angeline brought them out steaming cups of hot cocoa and they snuggled together in a blanket on her lounge chair hugging the hot drink to keep warm. The autumn air was definitely winning the battle against the summer heat as September came to an end. Kate shivered as she thought about the end of summer and moved in closer against Ben's warm body wrapped around her. She sipped her cocoa and leaned her head against his chest. That peaceful calm feeling was coming back to her. The waves crashed on the beach in the darkness and every so often the wind would carry a slight sprinkle of salty mist up to her face. She had everything she could ever want at that moment—it was perfection.

Ben leaned down and kissed the top of her head. He stroked her hair and said quietly, "You asked me earlier why I didn't quit my job years ago, since I hated it so much."

"Yes?" said Kate wondering where this was leading.

"You were right. I really hated it. In fact I hated it so much, that I was seriously thinking of taking the bastard's money and quitting after I got that letter from my dad's lawyer, you know? I was going to take the money and run, but then something happened that changed it all for me."

"What?" she whispered.

"I swear, the day I was going to give Hank my notice, some woman walked in the door of our shop. I shouldn't say 'some woman'. She was far from that. She was the most beautiful woman I'd ever seen in my life. Hank introduced her as, Kate, our new sales rep. That was it. I knew I could never leave...not as long as she was there."

Kate pulled away from him enough so she could see his face. "You mean...?"

"Yeah..." he said and hesitatingly proceeded. "I knew the moment I saw you." He looked away from her and out into the dark expanse of space before them. "Of course, then Tom showed up one day at work, and that was it for you." He laughed nervously. "I knew you were never going to fall for a guy like me. And since Tom was my best friend, at least I could keep you close...as long as you were close to him." He turned his gaze back to her and continued, "That was good enough for me...to be near you...to feel you take my breath away every time you walked into the room."

Kate struggled for a response, but he couldn't stop to allow her to speak at that point. He was on a roll, and he continued on.

"You took my breath away, Kate," he confessed. ""I know, I sound like a girl."

Kate smiled at his obvious embarrassment. He took it as a cue to continue with his confession. "And you know, after a while, you get used to not being able to breathe. You learn to live with a little less oxygen. It's worth it just to see her and study her...the way her mouth moves as she speaks, the childlike habit she has of tucking her hair behind her ear, and the way she closes her eyes and smiles just before she lets out a little laugh at some joke someone just told her. And as I said, eventually you grow accustomed to it, and you don't even notice anymore that you're not breathing. It becomes so natural to deprive yourself while you...simply...take...her...in. Because you know without her there, what's the point in breathing anyway?"

Kate felt tears streaming down her cheeks. Her face grew warm and red as he revealed this truth to her. "My God, Ben, I never realized."

"Yeah...well..." was all he could think of to say. "I never planned on telling you, but then this afternoon happened and I thought *what the hell*." He looked back at her and placed several gentle kisses upon her mouth.

"I never realized until this afternoon how I felt about *you*." Kate assumed her earlier position snuggled up against his chest. "Funny how things happen, isn't it?" she asked. "The things we think we should have…the people we think we should be with…but life has different plans…I have been quite surprised where life has led me."

Ben laughed. "Bet you never imagined you could love someone like me, huh?"

"Quite the contrary," said Kate. "I couldn't imagine love with anyone *but* you."

She looked up at him and squeezed Ben's hand, then their fingers intertwined, and Ben brought them up to his lips. "And the lavender roses? How did you know?" She asked quietly.

His eyes glazed with tears as he said, "I knew, because I love you, Kate."

"I love you too, Ben," she said. It felt blissful to finally say it.

Ben's emotions caught up with him. He choked on his tears as he said, "I wish I could go with you."

Upon hearing this, her own river of emotion flowed rapidly down her cheeks. "I don't want to leave you," she whispered. "I've only just now found you."

"That's not true," he said. "I've been here for a long time—right by your side." He wiped the tears from his eyes, frustrated by the pain he was feeling. He pressed his lips to her forehead. "We've had years together, and I enjoyed every minute of it. Remember the Painted Desert? You were so beautiful sitting out there with the wind blowing your hair. Your eyes sparkled in amazement at the wonder you were experiencing. And you were so incredibly strong as you told me the hardest thing you would ever have to say to anyone. I felt so honored to share that moment with you, Kate. It was awesome! And as miserable as it was for you, I thanked God that I was the one who got to go through it with you. We had everything—love, hate, joy, pain, and some of the best barbecue in the world." He laughed through his tears. He kissed her again and looked out at the sea.

She laughed too, but her body was tired. She rested her head against his chest and closed her eyes. "I guess you're right. We did have each other. I just didn't realize it." She pictured them both out in the desert, marveling at the colors and the magnificence that lay all around them. She knew she was leaving, but it didn't scare her anymore. A warm breeze drifted over her face just as it did that day in the desert. An overwhelming serenity wrapped around her that was stronger than even Ben's embrace. She could feel his heart pounding and the rushing sound of his blood as it coursed through his veins. She could feel herself slipping away, and at the same time, becoming larger and more a part of him. That's when she realized she wasn't actually saying goodbye. She was in his blood, in his breath, and in his thoughts. The sensation was strange, but at the same time so wonderfully familiar.

"He's more myself than I am. Whatever our souls are made of, his and mine are the same." Catherine's words from her beloved film, *Wuthering Heights,* came to her mind as this sensation enveloped her. She smiled.

It was then that she let go.

www.ingramcontent.com/pod-product-compliance
Lightning Source LLC
Chambersburg PA
CBHW051844170626
46807CB00003B/1334